X

KT-599-078

15 APR 2024

03785154 - ITEM

SPECIAL MESSAGE TO READERS

This book is published under the auspices of

THE ULVERSCROFT FOUNDATION

(registered charity No. 264873 UK)

Established in 1972 to provide funds for research, diagnosis and treatment of eye diseases. Examples of contributions made are: —

A Children's Assessment Unit at Moorfield's Hospital, London.

•

Twin operating theatres at the Western Ophthalmic Hospital, London.

•

A Chair of Ophthalmology at the Royal Australian College of Ophthalmologists.

•

The Ulverscroft Children's Eye Unit at the Great Ormond Street Hospital For Sick Children, London.

You can help further the work of the Foundation by making a donation or leaving a legacy. Every contribution, no matter how small, is received with gratitude. Please write for details to:

THE ULVERSCROFT FOUNDATION,
The Green, Bradgate Road, Anstey,
Leicester LE7 7FU, England.
Telephone: (0116) 236 4325

In Australia write to:
THE ULVERSCROFT FOUNDATION,
c/o The Royal Australian and New Zealand College of Ophthalmologists,
94-98 Chalmers Street, Surry Hills,
N.S.W. 2010, Australia

PACK RAT

When Wesley Roach scalps and kills old-timer Pack Rat Dan, Jack Carson vows revenge. He little realises that he faces Roach and his gang of gunslicks, the local marshal and, worst of all, the notorious Canyon Kate. Riding for a rival outfit and teamed with the oddball Tombstone, Carson is forced on the run. Meanwhile, his boss's daughter Laura disappears. Will Carson come face to face with his target? And how much lead must fly before he does?

COLIN BAINBRIDGE

PACK RAT

Complete and Unabridged

LINFORD
Leicester

First published in Great Britain in 2010 by
Robert Hale Limited
London

First Linford Edition
published 2012
by arrangement with
Robert Hale Limited
London

The moral right of the author has been asserted

Copyright © 2010 by Colin Bainbridge
All rights reserved

British Library CIP Data

Bainbridge, Colin.
  Pack Rat.- -(Linford western library)
  1. Western stories.
  2. Large type books.
  I. Title II. Series
  823.9'2–dc23

  ISBN 978–1–4448–0984–8

**EAST SUSSEX
COUNTY LIBRARY**

03785154	
ULV	31-JAN-12
WES	£8.99
CRO 1/21	RYE 9/12

1

Jack Carson came over the ridge on the big Appaloosa and saw the old man sprawled face down in the snow. There was a gaping wound in his back and he had been scalped. Carson was pretty sure that no Indian had done it and there was only one white man he knew who made a practice of it — Wesley Roach. Carson had come across him down Chihuahua way. At that time Roach had been pulling in a hundred dollars for a male scalp, fifty for a female. That was the sort of person he was. Furthermore, this bore the hallmark of his handiwork, the oldster's ears having been removed as well. It was that extra indignity which particularly enraged Carson.

But Wesley Roach hadn't been the only one. Although they had been dusted over, there were still traces of

1

horses' hoofs in the snow. Two of them.

And then there was the mule. Old Betsy wouldn't be riding any more trails either.

He had met the old man only a few days before. At that time Carson had been in a bad way. Coming down from the high country, his horse had slipped in a snowdrift, breaking its leg and leaving him no option but to shoot it. That left him a long ways from anywhere, having to make his way on foot. He had walked all day, making slow progress, sinking into snow up to his knees. When darkness came he had made camp in the shelter of an overhang, waking up in the night to the cold and desolation. Next day he had stumbled on. The landscape was obliterated by snow and he found it difficult to pick out any landmarks. Towards the middle of the day the wind began to gather strength and what had been flurries of snow developed by dark into a raging blizzard. All through that night he had sheltered as best he could in a grove of trees and before dawn set out once more. His strength was waning and he knew he could not last much longer. All he wanted to do was to sit down and rest but he knew he must drive himself on. If he stopped, he would not come round again. But it was one thing to know that and another thing to put it into effect. Exhausted and debilitated, he had lain down in the shelter of a rock. Though he was almost frozen, he began to feel a warm drowsiness overcome him. It was good. There was no need to struggle any more.

When he came round it was to find he was lying on something soft which was not snow but a mattress. Firelight flickered. He was lying in the back of a cave. Heaving himself up on one elbow, he saw a figure sitting beside the fire towards the entrance to the cave, which presently got to its feet and came towards him. It was the old man and he was carrying a bowl of strong hot broth.

'Here, take this,' the oldster said. 'It'll

warm you through.' Carson took the proffered bowl and swallowed a mouthful. He shivered and shook his head.

'That sure is good,' he said. The broth had been laced with whiskey and he could feel the concoction burning its way down his throat.

'This sure ain't the weather to be wanderin' about without a hoss,' the oldster said.

'Nope. Don't reckon I'll be tryin' it again real soon.'

The oldster held out a gnarled hand.

'Name's Dan,' he said. 'Folks tend not to call me that, though.'

'What do they call you?'

'Pack Rat,' he said. 'Don't sound too flatterin' but I've kinda got used to it. I guess it's on account of I done a lot of tradin' in my time.'

'Jack Carson,' Carson replied. 'And I sure appreciate the hospitality.' He finished the broth and made to move but the oldster restrained him.

'Take it easy,' the oldster said. 'Rest up awhiles.'

He moved to the fire and Carson lay back. It was warm in the cave and he was so tired.

When he came round again the cave was lighter and a ray of sun fell on the wall over his head. The embers of a fire still glowed but there was no sign of the old man. For the first time he saw that there was a mule tethered to a rock. Getting to his feet, Carson walked across and stroked it. He went to the cave mouth and looked outside. It was a glorious morning. Sunlight glanced off the snow and there were blue shadows. He sat down, warming himself at the still-glowing ashes. Presently he saw the old man coming towards him carrying a pile of birch branches and brushwood.

'I see you've made the acquaintance of old Betsy,' he said.

'She sure seems a fine girl,' Carson replied.

'You're right there. Me and Betsy bin together a long time. Rode a lot of trails.'

The old man threw the wood into a corner of the cave.

'Coffee?' he said.

It was black and strong and they ate pemmican with it.

'It ain't much,' the oldster said. 'Supplies is beginnin' to run low. Reckon I won't be needin' to pick any up, though, when I get to town.'

'Why's that? You fixin' to settle down?'

'Sure am. I bin up in those hills prospectin' for too long. Got me enough now to grubstake me an' old Betsy for a long whiles.'

The oldster looked over his mug at Carson.

'What about you?' he asked.

'Me? Bin ridin' shotgun for the Silver Valley line. Had about enough. Figured I'd head south, go back to ranchin' for a time.'

'You'll need a hoss. Nearest town is Riverton. Walkin', you could be there by noon tomorrow.'

'You headin' that way?'

6

'Ain't sure. Figure I'll just set right here for a few days, sort of get my bearings. After that, I reckon I'll head for Silver Junction. Nice town. Guess you must know it.'

Carson nodded. It was where he had been taken on by the stagecoach company.

'Well, Dan,' he said. 'I reckon I've taken up enough of your time.' He got to his feet.

'Say, why don't I pick out a few supplies for you down in Riverton? By way of payment for what you've done for me.'

'It's OK,' the old man said. 'You don't need to do that.'

Carson turned and stroked old Betsy.

'Figure she would have no objections to some extra feed,' he said.

'Well,' the oldster grinned, 'since you put it that way.'

Carson took him by the hand.

'Straight down the mountain,' the old man said. 'Bear left when you reach a clump of rocks. You can't go too far wrong.'

'So long,' Carson said.

He started down the mountain slope. When he had gone a short way he turned to see the oldster standing at the entrance to the cave. Behind him, he could just make out the shape of the mule. He waved an arm in acknowledgement. He would be back in a day or two. It was the last he saw of Pack Rat Dan.

He buried the old man near the entrance to his cave. He found a smooth rock and with the point of his knife he inscribed the words:

Dan. An old timer. Retired early.

He knew there was no point, but he checked the saddle-bags old Betsy had been carrying. There was nothing. Whatever gold the old man had found had been taken. Then he sat down in the mouth of the cave to think things over. It shouldn't take him long to catch up with Roach. He would have made for the nearest town of any size to blow some of his new-found wealth. That would probably be Silver Junction. He might have to shelve his plans for a time but it made little difference. He was under no obligations. First and foremost, there was the old man to be avenged.

★ ★ ★

It was dark when he hit Silver Junction. After leaving his horse at the livery stable, he made for the nearest hotel and checked in. Coming downstairs, he ate in the dining room and then glanced at the hotel register. There was no Wesley Roach. He might have been using a false name. He wandered out into the street and walked to the saloon, hoping he might just be lucky enough to find Roach there, but that would have been too easy. The place was quiet; some men were playing faro at a corner table and a few others were standing at the bar. He returned to the hotel, hung his guns over the headboard and for the first time in a long while enjoyed the comforts of a bed.

The next morning he made his way to the marshal's office.

'I'm looking for a man named Roach,' he said. 'Wesley Roach.'

The marshal looked him up and down.

'Wesley Roach?' he said.

'That's right. Thought you might have a dodger on him.'

'What? You some kind of bounty hunter?'

Carson shook his head. 'Nope,' he said. 'It's more personal.'

The marshal continued to observe him closely.

'He killed somebody, a friend of mine. If you like, I can take you to the spot.'

'None of my business,' the marshal said. 'Outside of my jurisdiction.'

'Yeah. I figured that.'

The marshal slowly rose to his feet and came round the table at which he had been seated so he was standing next to Carson.

'I keep a nice tidy town,' he said. 'I'd

hate to think either you or this Roach *hombre* might do anything to spoil that.'

'Want me to check in my guns?'

'Nope. I want you out of here.'

Carson started towards the door. As he reached for the handle, the marshal spoke again.

'I ain't got no dodger on Wesley Roach. He's been too clever for that. So far.'

Carson turned back.

'You know him?'

'Scalphunters are the lowest of the low. If you got no objection to hard ridin' you might try Wyoming. Ever been near a place called Crow Bend?'

Carson shook his head.

'You might find it suits you. Look out a little establishment called the Bird Cage. Seems like I heard somewhere this Wesley Roach has an understanding with the proprietress, a lady name of Canyon Kate. Personally, I'd as soon face up to a grizzly bear.'

Carson smiled. 'Thanks for the

11

information,' he said.

'It's a long ways. Seems like you're goin' to a lot of trouble.'

'It's no trouble,' Carson said.

Carson paid his hotel bill. No point in hanging about. It looked like he was in for some travelling. Once he got to Crow Bend there was no guarantee that he would find Roach there. But it was all he had to go on and if the marshal was correct, it seemed a likely place for Roach to make for. Especially with the old man's gold burning his pockets.

★　★　★

He hadn't ridden but two days out of town when he found the body. The man had been shot in the back. There was no sign of his horse and, after examining the ground, Carson reckoned it had simply been turned loose. Carson had a strong hunch that this was Roach's handiwork again, that Roach had murdered his companion for his share of the loot. He had shown some consideration for the victim; his hair was still intact. Carson's first instinct was to bury the remains and then he thought of the old man. Let the buzzards and the coyotes have him.

The days passed and Carson carried on riding. The land was empty and he met few other riders. Several times his path was crossed by a party of Blackfoot but they presented no threat. They were hunting the ever-dwindling herds of buffalo. At night he listened to the wind and the howling of the wolves and watched the constellations wheel across the vault of the heavens.

He calculated to be only about one day out of Crow Bend. The trail sloped gradually uphill and as he topped the rise he perceived a cloud of dust caused by a horse and buggy still some distance away. At first he thought nothing of it but then he heard a faint scream and with it came the realization that the horse was out of control. Applying his spurs to the Appaloosa's flanks, he set off at a gallop to try to head it off. Although the buggy was rattling on at speed it was no match for the Appaloosa and fairly quickly Carson had made up the ground and was closing in on the runaway rig. He was coming on it fast from the side and preparing to reach for the reins when it hit some obstruction in its path. For a few seconds it carried on, wavering crazily on two wheels before crashing over on its side, dragging the braying horse with it. One wheel flew into the air while the other remained spinning wildly. Quickly Carson jumped from the saddle. The occupant of the buggy lay in a crumpled heap among the wreckage. It was a young woman expensively dressed in a riding habit and high boots. She had been wearing a hat but it had flown loose to reveal her long auburn hair, Carson feared the worst, but to his relief she began to move.

'Take it easy,' he said, kneeling down beside her.

She had raised herself on one elbow.

He put his arms around her shoulder to support her.

'Do you hurt anywhere?' he asked.

She looked into his face. He couldn't help but notice her eyes were green.

'Just about all over,' she replied.

'Wait a moment,' Carson said.

He stepped to his horse and drew a flask from his saddle-bag.

'Here,' he said. 'Take a pull.'

He held the flask to her lips and she swallowed a drop of the whiskey it contained. She grimaced but the shot seemed to do her some good.

'I know it ain't maybe the polite thing to do,' Carson said, 'but I figure the circumstances are exceptional.'

In reply, she reached up and took another swig. She began to sit upright and then, with some support from Carson, she got to her feet and began dusting herself down.

'How do you feel? Are you sure you're OK?'

She nodded her head.

'I'm just shook up,' she replied.

She looked about at the wreckage of the buggy. The horse had struggled to its feet but remained trapped by the broken harness. Carson stepped forward to release it, stroking it while he did so.

'Is he injured?' she asked.

'He'll be OK.'

'I don't know what got into him. Something must have scared him.' She walked over to join Carson. 'You must forgive me,' she said. 'I haven't thanked you for your help. My name is Laura, Laura Routledge. My father is Caleb Routledge. He owns the Bar X.' The way she said it, it seemed she expected Carson to have heard of it.

'Name's Carson,' he said. 'I'm new around here. On my way to Crow Bend. Glad to meet you.'

They both looked at one another and suddenly she burst into laughter.

'Well,' she said. 'I must look a sight.'

Carson hesitated. 'Where is this Bar X?' he said. 'I guess we'd better get you back there.'

'I'll be fine,' she said. 'Don't worry. One of the hands will be along soon. I don't want to put you to any more trouble.'

'You won't be. Just let me fix a line to your old hoss. I hope you won't mind ridin' up on the Appaloosa with me? Is there anything you might want out of the buggy?'

Having secured the horse he climbed into the saddle and then reaching down, took her hand and swung her up in front of him.

'Just point us in the right direction,' he said.

He let the horse go at its own pace. The country was good and soon they came upon grazing cattle carrying the Bar X brand. There was no sign of any of the ranch hands. Carson commented on this.

'Roundup,' she said. 'They're out gathering strays from the brush country.' A thought struck her. 'We're a bit short,' she said. 'I don't know how you're fixed, but I'm sure my father

17

could find a job for you if you're interested.'

Suddenly her eyes glazed over and she swayed. Carson grabbed her and held her steady. She looked at him and then her eyes closed. She had fainted. There was nothing much he could do but carry on in the direction she had indicated and he was soon rewarded by his first glimpse of the Bar X ranch. It was a long, low building with wings built in a Spanish hacienda style. Behind it were various outbuildings and to the right of the yard stood the bunkhouse. There was still no one around but as he rode up to the hitch rail the door flew open and a middle-aged man with a close beard flecked with white appeared, flanked by a younger clean-shaven man. They both carried rifles.

'What happened to Laura?' the older man barked.

'She had an accident with the buggy. I was ridin' by,' Carson answered.

The two exchanged glances and then

the older man ran forward.

'Clem! Clancy!' he shouted.

A couple of cowboys ran out of the bunkhouse. Between them, they lifted Laura from the Appaloosa and carried her into the house. Carson stepped out of the leather.

'Take the horses to the stable,' the man said. 'See that they're attended to.'

He turned to Carson. 'Sorry about the artillery,' he said. 'You can't be too sure these days.' He proffered his outstretched hand. 'Name's Routledge,' he said, 'Caleb Routledge.'

He turned as if to introduce the other man but he had gone back inside the house.

'Come in. I reckon you could put away some grub and the cook's right on the job.'

They went inside. The room was comfortable, with a leather sofa and armchairs. Although it was not cold, a fire burned in a big open grate.

'Take a seat,' Routledge said. 'I'll be with you in a few minutes.'

He passed through to a bedroom where they had taken Laura. There was a discussion and then to Carson's relief he heard Laura's voice. Presently Routledge reappeared.

'She's come round,' he said. 'Rik's ridin' into town for the doc but I think she's gonna be OK.'

'Rik?'

'Sorry, that's her brother, my son. I was going to introduce you on the veranda.'

'Can I see Laura?'

'I don't see why not. Better not tire her, though.'

'I won't,' Carson said.

He went through to the bedroom. Laura was in bed with her head propped up on a pillow.

'Hello,' she said. 'Sorry I passed out on you. Guess I must have taken a bump to the head.'

'Do you feel all right now?'

'Sure. Still a bit shook up but nothing to worry about. My father is too fussy.'

'Maybe so, but it won't hurt to have

you checked out.'

'Think about what I said,' she concluded. 'I don't know what your plans are, but my father could sure use someone round the place just about now.'

Carson couldn't be certain whether or not she had spoken to her father, but later, as they sat in the lounge, Caleb Routledge brought the matter up himself. Over the meal, he had expressed his thanks once again for Carson's part in rescuing his daughter, and as they relaxed over a glass of bourbon and a cigar he asked Carson what his plans were.

'I ain't too sure,' Carson replied. He didn't want to say anything about Roach or the old man. 'I guess I'm sorta between jobs. Figured I'd head on down this way, see what turned up.'

'Have you experience of ranchin'?' Routledge asked.

'Sure have. It's what I bin doin' most of my life.'

'Then there's a job here if you want

it. It's a busy time and to be honest I'm short of hands.'

Carson had already had time to think things over. There was no guarantee that he would soon find Roach. If the marshal back at Silver Junction was correct, it seemed a fair bet that Roach might turn up at some stage. Carson had money but it wouldn't last indefinitely. All in all, it appeared to make good sense to take up Routledge's offer.

'That's mighty decent of you,' he replied. 'I'd be glad to accept.'

Routledge poured him another drink. 'Good,' he said. 'Then it's settled. When do you want to start?'

'I could do with a day or two,' Carson replied. 'I'd like to take a look at Crow Bend. How far is it into town?'

'Only about ten miles. Take the track behind the bunkhouse. It joins the main trail about four miles down the road. Report to Rik when you get back. He's acting as my foreman. When you've finished your drink I'll take you over to the bunkhouse. It'll be good to have you on board.'

★ ★ ★

The following morning after breakfast he set out for Crow Bend. The trail was as easy to find as Routledge had said it would be. When he arrived, he fastened his horse to the nearest hitch rack. Crow Bend was a small burg, not much bigger than Silver Junction, so the Bird Cage was easy to find. He had expected to find the usual tawdry saloon so he was taken aback when he came through the batwings. It was not like any saloon he had seen before in a small town. There were heavy-pile carpets, brocaded sofas, cut-glass chandeliers and a stained-glass ceiling. In one corner stood a gold-plated piano with candelabra. At the far end of the room a plush bar was backed by an ornate ormolu mirror. A few men were drinking at the bar but otherwise the place seemed deserted.

23

Carson strode to the bar and ordered a whiskey. The bartender poured him a glass and then stood the whiskey bottle on the table. Nobody seemed to take any interest, but Carson had the feeling that someone was watching him. He poured himself another drink from the bottle. At the far corner of the room there was a staircase leading up to the next floor. He felt that whoever was observing him was doing so from that vantage point and his hunch was proved right when he heard the sound of muffled footsteps on the thick carpet of the stairs and the swish of a heavy skirt. Without turning his head, he let his eyes glance in that direction. Coming into view was a very buxom woman. She wore a red velvet gown and in her dark wavy hair was a magnificent red feather. As she reached the bottom step the other people in the room seemed to acknowledge her with a faint deference. She entered the saloon and came slowly towards the bar. Carson could smell her rich scent like wind-blown jasmine on a soft southern night. She came right up to the bar and stood next to Carson. For a moment or two there was silence and then Carson became conscious of a kind of pressure to be the first to speak. Touching his hat, he half-turned and said:

'Howdy ma'am. Can I offer you a drink?'

'That would be nice,' she said.

Pointedly ignoring the bottle standing on the bar, she turned to the barman.

'My usual, Brannigan.'

While the barman served her, Carson took the opportunity to observe her more closely. She was wearing a bustle which accentuated her lavish figure and it was with something of an effort that Carson strove to avoid looking too closely at her huge breasts which the low-cut dress made a poor effort of concealing. In contrast to her features, which were lined and heavily made-up, the skin of her chest and shoulders looked remarkably white and smooth.

Despite the wrinkles and the make-up she was still a good-looking woman. About thirty years ago, Carson calculated, she must have been a beauty.

When the barman had poured her drink, she took a long sip of it before turning to Carson.

'I don't recall seeing you in here before,' she said. 'Are you new in town?'

'I guess so, ma'am,' Carson replied.

'Just passing through?'

'Not necessarily. In fact, might be around for awhiles.'

'And this is the first place on your itinerary?'

Carson shrugged. He became aware that the others were watching them surreptitiously.

'Well, I think I can understand that. A man has been out on the trail for a time, he needs a little refreshment.'

Carson swallowed the rest of his drink.

'Sure nice to meet you ma'am,' he said. 'But right now I got business to attend to.'

'Well, that's fine. You do whatever you have to do and come right back when you've finished. Just ask right along for Kate. That's me. Whatever you want, I think I can provide it.' She broke into a little low laugh. 'Who knows, I might even take a personal interest.'

'Why thank you, ma'am,' Carson replied. Again he touched his hat before turning to the barman.

'How much do I owe you? Mine and the lady's.'

He was about to reach into his pocket when she placed a hand on his arm.

'This time it's on the house,' she said.

Carson made his way to the batwings and stepped out into the sunlight. He had met Canyon Kate and it seemed like the Bird Cage opened all hours. Yet the place was almost deserted. OK, it was early. No doubt the place got livelier later in the day. But those furnishings must have cost a load and she looked like a lady with expensive

27

tastes. How did she make a living in a town like this? And Kate herself! She was a whole heap of woman and would take some handling. He remembered what the marshal back in Silver Junction had said about Roach having an understanding with her. He had assumed the marshal meant she was Roach's woman. Having met her, it didn't seem likely, and not because of her age. It needed some thinking about.

2

There was a checker game going on in the bunkhouse involving Clem and Clancy. Another cowboy had joined them, a young man named Lou Reynolds. A few others had come in from the range. Carson was lying back on his bunk when the door opened and Rik Routledge came in.

'I need someone to join Tombstone tomorrow,' he said.

There was no response.

'I'm looking for a volunteer.'

There was still no response. It seemed to Carson that the men were avoiding making eye contact with Routledge.

'OK,' Routledge said.

He turned to Carson.

'How about you?'

Carson raised himself on one elbow.

'Sure,' he replied. 'Tell me who he is

29

and where I find him?'

'He's out at the line shack on the lower range. He might be an awkward cuss to work with but he's good with stock.'

He turned to address the bunk house at large. 'We're doing all right with the range cattle,' he said. 'Tomorrow I want you boys to start working the breaks.'

Without further ado, he walked out of the bunkhouse. Clem got up from the table where he was playing checkers and came over to Carson's bunk.

'Reckon you drew the short straw,' he said. 'That's pretty wild country out there.'

'Yeah? I rode rough country before.'

'Not with someone like Tombstone,' one of the cowboys said. 'Man, he's more ornery than an old mossyhorn. Figure he's been out there so long he's started to turn into one.'

There was a burst of laughter before Clancy intervened.

'Old Tombstone ain't so bad. It all depends on whether he takes to you or not. Last one tried to spend any time with him just up and quit after a few days.'

'How are things fixed out there?' Carson said.

'There's all the grub you'll want and a good head of horses in the corral.'

'Sounds fine to me,' Carson said.

Thinking about it later, it seemed a good option. Out at the line shack he would be able to think things over. It would provide time for Roach to show his hand, if he ever did. It would also give him a reason to avoid Laura. For some reason, he felt awkward about seeing her again.

* * *

Next morning Carson set off for the line shack, observing the terrain because he would be working it. There was a fair bit of timber in the bottoms and Carson reckoned it was down there where the going would get rough. After riding for a time, the Appaloosa pricked up its ears and shortly afterwards he saw the line cabin. It was made of rough-hewn cottonwood logs and nearby was a corral which should have contained the horses. There weren't any horses. Even without that, Carson would have known as he approached the cabin that something was wrong. Dismounting, Carson withdrew his rifle from its scabbard and approached the cabin on foot, watchful for any signs of movement. Reaching the door, he kicked it open and spun inside. The place was deserted but looked as though it had been recently occupied. There was an unmade bunk bed in one corner and the remains of a meal on a crude wooden table. It only took a moment for Carson to take in the scene. There was just the one room.

He went back out of the door and approached the corral. The ground was all churned up and the gate hung loose. He heard a low groan and then he saw a figure lying in the brush. Holding his rifle at the ready, he approached the man. He was lying face down and there was a nasty wound across the back of his skull. He had obviously been clubbed in the back of the head with a gun butt. Carson carefully turned him over. His chin was stubbled and he wore a black patch over his right eye. He looked about fifty but he might have been younger. His mouth sagged open to reveal a few isolated brown stumps. Carson guessed it was how he had acquired his nickname. The remaining teeth were like tombstones.

Carson returned to his horse and brought out the whiskey flask. Returning to the prostrate figure, he held the man up and was rewarded by a flickering of the left eye. He held the flask to the man's lips and tipped it up. Most of the whiskey dribbled down his chin but it seemed to do the trick. The eye opened once more and this time remained open.

'My head hurts like hell.'

'You've taken a knock,' Carson replied. 'Let's get you back on your feet and inside the cabin.'

Carson was about to offer his assistance when the man suddenly sat up.

'And who might you be?' he said.

'Name's Carson, Jack Carson. I've signed up for the Bar X. They sent me out to work with you.'

'I don't need anybody,' Tombstone replied.

'Yeah, sure looks like it,' Carson said.

The man got to his feet and began to stagger. Carson made as if to help him but he waved him aside.

'All right,' Carson said. 'I'll see you at the cabin if you can remember where it is.'

Making his way to where he had left the Appaloosa, he brought him round to a shed and set about making him comfortable. When he had finished he returned to the corral. Tombstone lay face down the same way he had found him. This time he braced himself, picked the man up and carried him back to the cabin. He dumped him on the tousled bunk and set about building a fire. It wasn't cold, but he thought it might help. By the time Tombstone came round again he had coffee brewing.

'What happened?' Tombstone said.

'Never mind. Just take this.'

Carson offered Tombstone a tin mug of strong black coffee. Tombstone drank, not seeming to mind that it was piping hot. He pulled himself up so that he was sitting on the edge of the bunk.

'That's good,' he said. 'I appreciate it.'

Finishing the coffee, he suddenly did a surprising thing. With a deft movement of his hand he removed the patch. The eye that was revealed looked perfectly normal.

'Experiment,' he said. 'Didn't work.' Seeing Carson's puzzled expression he began to explain. 'Who wears eye patches? Sailors of course. And why? Because otherwise it takes time for their eyes to adjust to the difference in light above and below decks. Thought I'd put it to the test. Inside and outside the cabin. You can see it gets kinda dark in here.'

That much was true. With the door closed and no windows, it was quite dim inside the cabin. Apart from that, Carson wondered whether his companion was affected by the blow to his head.

'Look here,' Tombstone said. He got to his feet, wincing with pain as he did so. He reached below the bunk and pulled out a box.

'My books,' he said. 'Wouldn't be without 'em. Get a chance to read once in a while out here. Wouldn't happen back at the bunkhouse.'

Carson moved over and knelt down. The books seemed to be mainly works on natural history and science and there was one battered encyclopaedia.

'Can't say I know too much about books,' he said.

Tombstone leaned down to slide the box back and at that point passed out once more. Carson decided to leave him where he was till he came round again. He bathed Tombstone's wound and wrapped a makeshift bandage round it. He took it as maybe something of a success that Tombstone had shown him his books. He picked one up and began to read.

When Tombstone had recovered, he told Carson in a few words what had happened. He didn't know too much about it. In the early hours he had been awakened by the snicker of a horse. He had run outside in time to see several figures gathered about the corral. He had run forward and then everything went blank. He could remember a blinding pain and seeing stars and then nothing.

'How many do you think there were?'

Carson had already examined the ground about the corral. He reckoned there had been half a dozen.

'I think I saw maybe three of 'em,' Tombstone said. 'It was dark. I'd just woke up. I wasn't really takin' things in.'

'Any idea who they might be?'

'Some.' He seemed reluctant to elaborate.

'Go on,' Carson said.

'Look, I don't want to make an issue of this. It ain't the first time I bin slugged from behind.'

They lapsed into silence.

'I'm feeling OK now,' Tombstone said after a while. 'How about we round up some steers?'

'How you gonna do that without a horse?' Carson said.

Tombstone smiled. 'I got me a horse,' he said. 'She's in the meadow behind the trees. She's like me; don't like to mix with the other broncs.'

They walked out behind the corral and through a bunch of cottonwoods. In the corner of a small field stood a skewbald quarter horse.

'Some folks reckon a mare is a bunch quitter. Not Cleo. Anyway, she don't run with the remuda except once as a bell mare.'

They rode out in the direction of the hills and, seeing some cattle, commenced to drift them. Like Rik had said, it was rough country. They rode into the brush to roust out the cattle that had taken up residence there, working hard to prevent them circling and getting back in. It was hard sweaty work but eventually they had about twenty head of cattle which they started moving towards the cabin. A couple of old bulls kept trying to lead the others back but Tombstone rode them tight.

'There should be more,' Tombstone commented. 'There's plenty of sign but too many of those draws are empty.'

Carson leaned over the saddle.

'Couldn't be anything to do with those *hombres* who clubbed you and took the horses?' he said.

Tombstone seemed to think for a moment or two.

'Has Routledge said anything to you?' he asked.

'Routledge? Nope. What would he have said?'

'It ain't really my business but I guess you've a right to know. Seems like some of the cattle have been disappearin'.'

'Cattle rustling,' Carson commented. 'Any idea who's behind it?'

'There's no proof but there's suspicions. Ever hear of a man named Otis Griffin?'

Carson shook his head.

'No reason why you should. He's fairly new around these parts. Bought a big spread north of here, calls it the Slash H. There were some rumours flyin' around about how he came by it but I never gave them no mind. Folks are a mite nervous of his intentions. Seems he's bought up a few properties in town and is makin' nice with the marshal.'

'And he's leanin' on some of the ranchers?'

'Just gently. So far. But he's ambitious.'

'Stealin' a whole bunch of horses wouldn't be too discreet,' Carson said.

'Who knows? But he's been seen in some dubious company.'

★　★　★

Over the next few days Carson and Tombstone continued to roust out cattle from the breaks, bunching them in the corral at the end of the day. Tombstone proved to be a good brush-popper. It was no easy matter to drop a loop in the brush but Tombstone did it with unerring accuracy. Sometimes they worked together and sometimes they split up to work the canyons. At night they slept in the line cabin, too tired to talk and next daybreak rolled out, cooked breakfast and then climbed into leather once more. At the end of that time they had less than a hundred and twenty head of cattle and they both knew it should have been more. They worked them back to the ranch where they joined the rest of the herd that was gathering for the coming drive. It was Saturday and most of the boys were heading into town. Carson thought it might be a good time to pay another visit to the Bird Cage.

The place provided quite a contrast to when he had been in last. Now it was filled with cowboys. Some were talking to girls seated on sofas which were scattered about the room. Canyon Kate was at the bar and as he entered through the batwings she glanced round and acknowledged his arrival with a nod of her head. She came across to join him and they sat at one of the tables. The waiter arrived with drinks.

'Decided to take up my invitation?' she said.

'What invitation was that?'

'It's a standing one,' she said.

'So why me?'

'Oh, something about you. You kind of interest me.'

'Yeah? Well, I guess it ain't my good looks.'

'You don't look so bad,' she replied.

She took a sip from her drink, barely touching the glass with her painted lips. She was dressed in a similar fashion to the last time only this time the velvet dress was yellow and cut even lower. She wore a yellow feather to match. It seemed to suit the name of the establishment. She looked up again and examined Carson with a searching look.

'Lots of fellas come in here,' she said. 'They all act pretty much alike and that's because they're after the same thing. Now you, you strike me as being different. Maybe you'd like a girl, but that isn't the main reason you're here. Is it?'

Kate had caught him slightly off guard but he didn't see any reason why he should prevaricate.

'Do you know a man called Wesley Roach?' he said.

If he had thought to catch Kate out, it didn't work. She showed no sign of surprise whatever.

'Wesley Roach? Seems like it should be the kind of name to stick in your mind but I can't say it means anything to me. Why? Who is he?'

Carson was suddenly aware that they were leaning together. Kate's breasts were glistening in the lamplight and he was conscious of her scent. He sat back slightly in his chair.

'Don't matter,' he said. 'Just call him an acquaintance I ain't seen in a while.'

'I could ask around,' Kate replied.

'Don't worry. It was just a long shot.'

'There must be a reason why you thought I might know of him. Otherwise, why choose this place rather than any other?'

'I guess somebody just mentioned your name. Maybe it had nothing to do with Roach.'

'You say this man Roach is an acquaintance. You seem to be going out of your way to find someone who is merely an acquaintance.'

'Forget it,' Carson said.

'Well, now that you're here let me just ask the barman.' She looked over at the bar. In a trice the barman was at her side. 'Brannigan,' she said. 'Perhaps you can help this gentleman. He's making enquiries about a man named Wesley Roach. That was the name, wasn't it?'

'Yes, but it's really not worth botherin' about.'

She turned to Brannigan. 'Does the name mean anything to you?'

The barman thought for a moment. 'No ma'am,' he concluded.

'That's fine,' she said, 'but keep your ears open and let me know if you do hear anything.'

'Yes ma'am,' he replied. He made his way back to the bar.

'Well Mr Carson,' Kate said. 'I've enjoyed talking to you again but I'm sure you've got other things on your mind apart from this Roach business. Perhaps a girl? Whatever your taste, I think I can provide someone suitable.'

'Maybe later,' Carson said.

'Just let me know. Take your time, enjoy yourself. Take a look at the merchandise.'

With a smile, she rose and made her way to one of the other tables. The piano began to play. Carson looked across the smoke-filled room at the bar. There was no sign of the bartender Brannigan. Suddenly the place, which had seemed richly decorated and ornate, appeared shoddy. Carson continued to observe the bar. Presently

Brannigan reappeared. Carson was suspicious. He looked at Kate. She was laughing with one of the customers. She didn't look back and appeared unconcerned. Carson stood up and as he turned away one of the girls took his arm. Despite her crude make-up she was pretty and under other circumstances he might have been tempted.

'Buy me a drink?' she said.

Carson obliged and they took a seat. Carson looked her over. The paint made her look older. Underneath, he could see that she was quite young. She had large dark eyes and her hair was done up in brown ringlets. Her tight-fitting satin dress did a good job of displaying her curves.

'You don't say much,' she said.

Carson had still been thinking about the bartender. Now he gave the girl his attention. Hell, she was real pretty and he had been a long time in the saddle.

'Is there somewhere we could go?' he said.

The girl smiled. 'Of course. Come with me.'

When they stood up she took his arm again. They wandered across the room and began to climb the stairs. At the top there was a corridor with rooms leading off at regular intervals. She stopped outside one and opened it with a key, closing it when they were inside. The room was sparsely decorated, mainly just a bed and a bedside table. Starlight gleamed through a closed window. There were none of the trappings of the room downstairs.

'Why don't you make yourself comfortable,' the girl said.

She took the bow out of her hair and shook her hair down. Carson sat on the bed. She began to undo the fastenings of her dress so that it slid down her body to the floor. Underneath she was wearing a purple satin basque and silk stockings. Carson approached her.

'Steady,' she said.

She moved her hands over his chest and slipped them down to his trousers.

'My,' she said. 'Looks like I got myself a real boy.'

She started to undo his belt. Carson moved back to the bed. Without undressing further she came and lay beside him, opening his shirt and running her fingers through his chest hair and then reaching down to his groin. Carson was finding it difficult to resist; if he was to ask her the question he had asked of Kate, he had to do it now.

'What do you know about a man called Wesley Roach?'

Her reaction was in marked contrast to Kate's. In an instant her dalliance was forgotten as she sat bolt upright. She was startled and looked confused.

'What do you mean?' she began. 'How do you — '

She stopped suddenly. Carson reached towards her and then he saw the key. Something registered in his brain. She had opened the door with the key but she had not locked it again. Why not? Then he found himself thinking of Brannigan. Why had he been absent from the bar? Carson looked at the girl. Her eyes were raised to his and there seemed to be a question in them.

'Kiss me,' she said, and at the same moment he thought he heard a sound outside, in the corridor or on the stairs. In an instant Carson was on his feet and reaching for his guns. They weren't there and then he remembered that he had checked them in when he entered the Bird Cage.

'What are you doing?' the girl screamed.

Carson looked swiftly round the room. There was no mistaking the sounds of footsteps outside in the corridor. They were running now and approaching the room.

'Sorry, ma'am,' he breathed and without hesitation he leaped forward and went crashing through the window. Glass shattered around him and the girl lying on the bed screamed once again. At the same instant the door burst open and two men dashed inside waving six-guns in the air. They looked at one another.

'Where is he?' one of them said and then they saw the shattered window. They ran across and leaned out. One of them raised his gun and fired a shot into the night. The other one grabbed his arm.

'Let's get down there. He can't have got far.'

Carson had leaped from the second storey. As he landed, he rolled over, wincing as a stab of pain seared across his ankle, but he was able to put his weight on it and, bent double, he ran pell-mell for an opening at the side of the saloon. He heard the shot ring out behind him as he thundered down the dark alley, thinking what a fool he had been. How could he have been so stupid? It was obvious now that he had been set up. Someone had set the trap and he had walked right into it.

Coming to the end of the alley, he drew to a halt before setting off down a short street which led to another narrow passage, emerging on to some broken-down shacks and disused corrals. He was panting for breath but reckoned that he was safe. Then his straining ears picked up the sounds of boots pounding along in his rear. He started off again, rounding the nearest corral and then running across a little wooden platform leading over a stream to some trees. The sounds of pursuit dwindled and he stopped to take stock of the situation. The night was quiet. Now and again the breeze picked up a faint tinkling sound — the piano still playing back at the Bird Cage as the batwings were opened and closed. Somewhere among the trees an owl hooted. But that was all. It was only then that he realized he was bleeding and, looking down, saw that the window glass had cut him across the shoulder where he had put his weight. There were other minor cuts and his foot felt sore from where he had landed on it. Otherwise, he was OK. Peering out from the shelter of the trees, he could see no sign of anyone. Quickly he made his way out of the copse and through the deserted streets and alleys back to the Bird Cage. He intended getting those six-guns back.

As he strode through the batwings a few people glanced up but quickly got back to what they were doing. Looking about him, he saw Canyon Kate at the bar talking to Brannigan and another man. She looked up but her face was immobile. As he moved forward, Carson saw Brannigan reach behind the bar but at a nod from Kate he straightened up. Kate said something to the other man she was talking with. He turned slightly and Carson saw that he wore a star on his waistcoat. As he came up Kate smiled.

'That was rather an unorthodox exit,' she said. She looked at Carson's shoulder, which was oozing blood. 'We didn't expect to see you again so soon.'

'I left my guns behind,' Carson said.

She laughed, a strange hollow sort of laugh, and turned to the marshal.

'This is the man I was telling you

about,' she said. 'I'm afraid I just can't countenance this sort of caper in my establishment.'

The marshal turned to Carson. He was young and sported a straggling moustache.

'You've got a nerve coming back,' he said. 'Still, it makes my job so much easier.' He whipped a gun from his holster. 'You're under arrest,' he said.

Carson realized there was nothing he could do. 'On what charge?' he said.

'Try disturbin' the peace, damagin' property, disorderly behaviour. You want me to go on?'

Carson shrugged.

'OK,' the marshal said. 'Put your hands in the air and you an' me'll take a little walk.'

The marshal gestured towards the street and Carson headed for the batwings. He glanced around but there was no sign of the girl. Maybe she was already with another client. Emerging from the cat-house, they crossed the road diagonally and kept on till they reached the marshal's office. There was a light on inside and at a knock on the door it was opened by a man wearing a deputy's badge.

'Another one?' he said.

'Yup. Put him in the lockup.'

The deputy picked up a set of keys as the marshal moved to the door.

'How long you figure to hold me?' Carson called.

'For as long as it takes,' the marshal replied.

As the marshal left, the deputy opened another door into a short corridor. At the end was a single jail cell and in the dim light falling through a high window Carson could see that it was already occupied. Pushing Carson inside, the deputy checked that the cell was locked and walked off, his boots ringing on the stone floor. The door to the marshal's office slammed shut and the place became even gloomier. Carson stood clutching at the bars for a few moments, his eyes trying to adjust themselves to the darkness. There was a shuffling sound behind him and then a voice spoke:

'That you, Carson?' He spun round.

'Tombstone! Why don't I feel surprised?'

3

'How the hell did you get here?' Carson said.

'Tell me your story and then I'll tell you mine,' Tombstone replied.

Wasting few words, Carson gave a brief version of what had happened to him.

'I said there were rumours about the marshal,' Tombstone commented. 'He certainly seems to have some original views on enforcin' the law.'

Tombstone told his tale. It seemed he had got into some kind of brawl with a man who'd made a comment about the Bar X.

'I figured he was another of Griffin's stooges,' he said. 'The marshal didn't waste a lot of time lookin' into the matter.'

'But what were you doing in town? I thought you were back at the line shack.'

'Well, I kinda got to thinkin' about a little matter of a knock on the head and some missin' hosses. Figured I might just get me a lead as to who could be responsible, maybe even get a sight of one of the critters in town. Matter of fact, I saw a blue roan that sure reminded me of one I had in the corral. Never got a chance to check it out though.'

Carson was silent for a moment. 'Question is,' he said, 'how do we get out of here? If it's down to the marshal, I reckon we could be in for a long stay.'

'Don't you worry about that,' Tombstone grinned. He reached into a pocket and produced a key.

'I was a bit worried in case they frisked me,' he said. 'This here key will open the door for us. I was just thinkin' about what to do with the marshal and his deputy once I walked free.'

Carson gave him a wondering glance.

'A place like this,' Tombstone said, 'won't present any problem. They'll have built it cheap and easy. That's a

57

warded lock. All it needs is a key with the warded section removed.'

'Somethin' else you got from your books?' Carson said. Tombstone grinned, revealing his few teeth.

'You realize,' he said, 'that once we walk out of here we'll be wanted men?'

'Yeah. Looks like the deputy's on duty tonight. We'll wait a while. Maybe he'll nod off.'

Talking stopped. After a time, the light vanished from beneath the door to the marshal's office but there was no sound of the outside door being closed.

'He must have turned down the lamp,' Carson said. 'Give him just a bit more time.'

The minutes passed. Finally Carson touched Tombstone on the shoulder.

'Let's see if that key works,' he said.

'It'll work.'

Tombstone extended his arm and reached through the bars of the prison door. Bending his hand round, he fiddled about for a moment until he felt the skeleton key slide into the lock. His hand was in an awkward position but he gently began to work the key in the lock. After a few moments there was a click and, withdrawing his hand, he pushed very gently on the door. It opened and he turned to Carson with a grin on his face. Carson motioned him to be silent, though it was difficult to make out anything much in the gloom. With Carson in the lead, they slipped through the open cell door and crept to the door which led into the marshal's office. They listened closely but could hear nothing. There was no indication of what the deputy was doing. Carson gently seized the door handle and pulled. Nothing gave. The door was locked!

'Deputy, there's a problem!' Carson shouted. 'This other hombre in here with me; I think he's dead.'

They heard a shuffling on the other side of the door.

'You'd better not be wastin' my time,' the deputy called.

Another moment passed and then

there was a rattle of keys and a fumbling at the lock. The door swung inwards and as it did so Carson launched himself at the figure beyond. Caught by surprise, the deputy muttered something and then he was hurled backwards by the weight of his attacker. Carson swung his fist and the deputy went down, smashing his head against the table leg as he went. Carson was on him, delivering another blow to the prostrate figure. He put his ear to the man's mouth.

'He's breathin' fine,' he said. 'He'll be all right.'

'Who cares? Let's get the hell out of here.'

Carson reached down and took the deputy's gunbelt, fastening it around his waist. On the wall there was a rack of rifles. He threw one to Tombstone and took another himself.

'Make for the Bird Cage,' he snapped.

The main door to the office was closed but it took only a matter of seconds for Carson to choose the right key from the deputy's chain. Opening the door, they burst into the deserted street and sprinted to the Bird Cage. There were horses tied to the hitch rack. Hoisting themselves into leather they wheeled away, their horses' hoofbeats echoing from the darkened clapboard buildings.

'Guess the marshal can add horse-thievin' to the list,' Tombstone yelled.

They passed quickly through the town and soon they were in open country. The landscape had a curious luminous quality. Clouds which had earlier covered the sky were broken now and the moon cast an eerie glow.

'Where to?' Carson shouted.

'Make for the line cabin.'

Once they were well clear of the town they slowed their horses down. They were back on Bar X land when Tombstone pointed ahead.

'Maybe I'm mistaken,' he said, 'but I thought I saw something.'

They strained their eyes. Carson

raised himself in the stirrups. Still he couldn't distinguish anything but presently the stillness of the night was broken by the lowing of a cow. Then they both saw the faint outlines of horses that were almost indistinguishable from the surrounding darkness.

'How many?' Carson said.

'Four men, I reckon. And some cow critters.'

The figures began to move slowly and a horse snickered in the distance.

'Rustlers!' Carson said.

'Sure seems that way.'

'What do you think? Do we do something about it?'

Tombstone grinned. 'Hell yes,' he said.

Taking their rifles out of their scabbards, they urged their horses to a gallop. Becoming aware that they had been detected, the rustlers started to ride away, the longhorns galloping alongside them. A shot rang out and suddenly the cattle split apart but the rustlers made no attempt to follow them. Tombstone raised his rifle and fired once in return but it was pointless, shooting in the dark. They were making some ground on the rustlers when they disappeared over the brow of a rise; when they came back into view they had divided their forces.

'OK!' Carson shouted. 'Leave it! Let them go!'

They reined in their mounts.

'There's nothing to be gained,' Carson said. 'We had a pretty good idea that someone was rustling Bar X cattle. At least that's a few less for 'em.'

Tombstone grunted.

'Let's head for the line cabin,' Carson said.

They rode the rest of the way without further incident. Leaving the horses in the corral, they went inside, lit a fire and made themselves comfortable. Tombstone produced a pouch of Bull Durham and they built themselves a smoke.

'I got to hand it to you,' Carson said. 'That key routine was somethin' special.'

Tombstone laughed. 'Got me that

idea from a catalogue,' he said. He stretched himself in front of the fire. 'You know, I bin around a long time, but I still remember one of the first winters I ever put in. I'd been sent out to an abandoned shack to make a line camp. It was in a bad state but it was papered with old newspapers and farm journals. Well, it got kinda lonesome out there for a young fella. There was nothin' to do so I set to readin' those old papers, startin' with the east wall and kinda workin' my way round to the west. I'd just started on the ceilin' when they called me back to the ranch.'

Carson laughed. 'So that's where it all started, your readin' an' all?'

'Sure was.'

'You ought to retire, go back east and enrol yourself in one of them dude colleges.'

'Yeah. Maybe you're right, especially now that barbed wire's changin' the old ways.'

Tombstone took another swallow of whiskey. He seemed to be getting expansive and Carson let him rattle on.

'Maybe some cowpoke would come back after a drive and bring a few yeller-backed novels along with him. Them books would go the rounds till they was plumb wore out. Then the boot and saddle makers and the mail-order houses started sendin' out their catalogues and the old bunkhouse library got started. Me, I wanted to know things and it was the catalogues really got me goin'. I used to burn the midnight oil thumbin' 'em through.'

'Guess it's lucky for me you did. I mean, you havin' that key.'

'That Bird Cage,' Tombstone said, going off at a tangent. 'I ain't bin there in a long time. Still, I can understand a young fella like you — '

'Yeah,' Carson interrupted, 'but I wasn't there for a girl. Not this time, anyway.'

'Is that so? Now why else might a body be makin' out at the Bird Cage?'

Carson hesitated. He had meant to keep the Wesley Roach business a private matter, but things had changed. Keeping it as brief as possible, he informed Tombstone of his interest in finding the oldster's murderer.

'This Roach sounds a mean son of a bitch,' Tombstone said. 'Always assumin' you're right about what he did to the old fella.'

'I'm right,' Carson retorted.

'You haven't got much to go on.'

'Maybe not, but it's enough.'

Tombstone scratched his head and blew out a cloud of smoke. The fire in the grate crackled and threw out a spark.

'You know,' he said, 'I'm kinda thinkin'. Don't you reckon it's a bit of a coincidence that you're here lookin' for this varmint Roach right along the same time there seems to be a bad outbreak of cattle rustlin'?'

'Yup. The thought had crossed my mind.'

'Maybe there's some sort of a tie-in.'

Carson nodded. 'What do you know about this man Griffin?'

'Just what I told you. He bought up the Slash H spread and since then he's been nosin' about town. He seems to have money but he's not averse to applyin' pressure. From what I heard, folks have been sellin' up for less than their properties are worth. They don't want trouble.'

'How long's Cobb been marshal?'

'Not long, just since old Marshal Gillespie turned in his badge after the accident.'

'Accident?'

'Came off his horse. The critter landed on top of him. Busted his leg. He was laid up for a while.'

'And Cobb took over? Now that's interestin'.'

'What are you thinkin'?'

'Could be Griffin's influence.'

'It would fit,' Tombstone said. 'And like I told you, there's some hardcases been seen around town ridin' with the Slash H outfit.' He paused. 'The sort of mean coyotes your man Roach might associate himself with.'

Carson was thinking hard. 'It sounds reasonable, but it's only guesswork. We need more proof. That girl at the Bird Cage, I'm sure she knows somethin'. I surprised her when I mentioned Roach's name just before those gunmen broke in on us. What I'd like to know is just what the connection is between Roach and Canyon Kate. Why would Kate go to the bother of tryin' to protect him?'

Tombstone blew out another cloud of smoke. 'What do you reckon the marshal's goin' to do when he finds we busted loose?'

'I don't know. He ain't got a whole lot to hold us on, but if Griffin's behind him he might decide to follow it up. After all, those *hombres* back at the Bird Cage weren't kiddin' about. And the marshal was talkin' to Canyon Kate when I came back.'

'The marshal don't know about the line cabin,' Tombstone said. 'Let's just carry on here and see if anythin' happens. Business as usual.'

'It might get interestin' back at the ranch,' Carson replied. 'Especially if Griffin's been leanin' on Routledge.'

'Routledge is a good man,' Tombstone said. 'I bin ridin' for him a long time. He won't buckle in to pressure.' He looked quizzically at Carson. 'And he's sure got a good lookin' daughter. She can get kinda frisky at times. I've knowed her since she was a kid. A good girl, but she can be headstrong. I understand you've made her acquaintance.'

'Yes,' Carson replied.

'And her brother. Two of a kind in some ways. He's very protective but maybe feels the need to prove himself. He can be abrasive. It don't pay to get on the wrong side of him.'

'Thanks for the advice,' Carson said, 'but I don't intend gettin' involved with Miss Routledge or her brother.'

'No, of course not,' Tombstone replied. 'You're just another cow puncher puttin' in his time.'

'Yeah. And once those cows are

rounded up I'll be hittin' the trail.'

'What about Roach?'

'Roach will get his,' Carson replied. 'There's no rush. Sooner or later I'll deal with him.'

* * *

The days passed and there was no sign of the marshal. The weather had turned hot and dry and it was harder than ever to drive the wild stock out of the breaks. When they had enough, Carson and Tombstone started them towards the roundup grounds. Their combings from the canyons and coulees were among the last to be driven in. As they headed for the bunkhouse they passed Routledge who had just been in conversation with two other ranchers who had agreed to pool their resources. Routledge summoned them over.

'Some of my boys have reported numbers of missing cattle. You've been out combing the breaks. What's your impression?'

They told him what they had seen on the night of the jailbreak.

'This needs thinkin' about,' Routledge said. 'I suspect Griffin is behind it but we can't be certain. I've told the boys to keep their eyes open. We'll need to take extra care protectin' the herd.'

He turned to Carson.

'Tombstone has been with me a long time. Same with most of the others. They have an allegiance. I think it's only fair that you be made aware of the situation here. Things could turn ugly. I would understand — '

'My bedroll's in the bunkhouse, my horse is in the remuda. When I signed I signed to the brand,' Carson interrupted.

'I thought you might say that. By the way, I gather you had a bit of a run-in with the marshal recently.'

'Yeah, I guess you could say that.'

'Well, it's no real business of mine. Take this as just a gentle warning. The marshal could make things hard for you.'

71

Carson and Tombstone walked away just as Laura came round the corner of the ranch house. It was good timing. Tombstone grinned and Carson had the feeling that she had been waiting for him.

'Well hello, Mr Carson,' she said as Tombstone left them.

'Hello, Miss Routledge.'

'Please, call me Laura. How are you finding things on the ranch?'

'Fine. Thanks again for putting in the word.'

'Oh, I didn't need to do that. Father can tell a good ranch-hand. I understand you've been working the breaks. That can get a little rough.'

'All part of the job,' he replied.

Laura looked away before speaking. 'I don't suppose you get much chance to go into town.' she said.

'Not much,' he replied.

'Some of the boys like to go in on a Saturday night. I don't know what they get up to, but whatever it is I suppose it helps blow off a little steam. Things can get very cramped on the ranch. I ought to know.'

'I think you're right,' Carson said. 'The boys work hard. They deserve a little relaxation.'

She looked up at him from under her hat. 'Good day, Mr Carson,' she said.

Carson watched as she walked away.

* * *

Carson and Tombstone ate with the rest of the hands in the bunkhouse. When they had finished they wandered across to the corrals where the remuda was gathered. It was another clear night. They could see for miles across the range and in the distance the hills were dimly outlined against the sky.

'Reckon there's any cows left up there among the foothills?' Carson asked.

'I think we about cleared them out,' Tombstone said. 'Leastways legitimate cattle.'

'What do you mean?'

'Well, if Griffin and his men are stealin' Bar X brand stock, where do you think he might keep 'em?'

'Dunno. Mixed in with the rest of the herd I guess.'

'Maybe so.'

'You're thinkin' they might be hidden somewhere?'

'Yup,' Tombstone replied. 'Like up among those peaks. There's plenty of places a few head of cattle might be pastured.'

Carson considered the suggestion, but not for long.

'Let's grab some rest tonight,' he said, 'and tomorrow we'll take a ride up into the hills.'

4

Early next morning they saddled up their horses and headed for the hills. Soon they were high above the valley. There wasn't much of a trail but as they rode they kept their eyes strained for any sign of cattle. Eventually they stopped to give their horses a chance to graze.

'This is a bit hit and miss,' Carson said. 'Maybe there's a more systematic way of doin' things.'

'We could maybe have got some of the boys involved,' Tombstone said, 'but we're short of hands. Anyway, we're only playin' a hunch.'

'Sure is nice up here though,' Carson said. 'A country like this makes a man kinda get the urge to settle down.'

'Yeah,' Tombstone said. 'It sure is pretty.'

They rode on and in the middle of

the afternoon, coming through a gap in the hills, saw another long vista below them. In the middle distance stood a big ranch house.

'The Slash H,' Tombstone said. 'Just about as far as you can see, that's Slash H land.'

'Sure is a big spread,' Carson said.

'If Griffin gets his way, it'll only be the start.'

They turned back. Evening shadows were filling the lower reaches of the hills and they had found no sign of Bar X cattle. A smudge of cloud hung low and it was only as they got near the line cabin that they smelled smoke and realized what it was.

'Fire!' Carson yelled.

They galloped forward but when they reached the line shack there wasn't much left of it. Instead, they were confronted with a burned-out ruin.

'Hell!' Tombstone muttered. 'They weren't content to run off some horses this time.'

He jumped down and began to

search among the smouldering remains, digging with his fingers among the ashes. Presently he held up the charred remnants of a book. 'Guess I won't be doin' much readin' for a while,' he said.

Carson started looking around. It wasn't difficult to find sign of a number of riders. Bending down to examine the ground where it was churned up by hoofs, he calculated there were half a dozen of them. The trail was plain to see and even though it was dark they had no problems following it. Soon it became apparent that it was leading towards town. They rode on, both grim and single-minded. Carson was carrying a .44 Winchester rifle and two Colt .44 pistols. Tombstone was carrying the same guns and in its scabbard an older Henry sixteen-shot repeater. If necessary, they were in the mood to use them.

It was late when they hit town. As usual, music and light spilled out through the batwing doors of the Bird Cage but the horses they were looking for were hitched outside the Crazy Nugget saloon. Climbing down from the leather, Carson and Tombstone tied their horses to the rack and examined the others for the Slash H brand. Nodding to each other, they entered the saloon. It was pretty full but immediately a hush fell upon the scene. People could see that they meant business. Standing at the bar were a number of cowboys. The barman looked up at their approach.

'Whose are those horses at the hitch rail?' Carson barked.

There was a tense pause. The barman finally spoke.

'There are a number of horses at the hitch rail.'

'The ones carryin' the Slash H brand.'

Again there was silence. The barman looked as though he was about to speak again when one of the cowboys at the bar turned slowly to face the newcomers.

'Who's askin?' he said.

Carson ran a glance over him. He was tough looking and he wore his six-guns low and tied with a thong. His leather waistcoat was grimy and bore traces of ash.

'Looks like you got yourself singed,' Carson said.

Involuntarily the man glanced down.

'We don't want any trouble,' the bartender began. 'Perhaps I could offer you gentlemen a drink?'

'No drink,' Carson said.

The man looked up again. There was anger in his eyes and his lips had drawn together tight. The drinkers at the bar had slowly moved apart leaving only a small bunch still standing where they had been. Five of them.

'I don't like your attitude,' the man said.

His five companions turned slowly so they were facing Carson and Tombstone. Carson was watching closely. The men were obviously not cowboys. From the way they carried themselves and the way they wore their weapons, they looked like men who were used to making a living out of their shooting skills. The six of them were slowly spreading.

'I don't like finding my cabin burnt out,' Tombstone snarled.

'I don't know what you're on about,' the gunman said.

'We think you do. But if you like to step across to the marshal's office we can sort this out. Let him decide who's right and who's wrong.'

The man emitted an ugly laugh.

'The marshal,' he said. Suddenly his face straightened and he spat on the floor.

'Sure,' he said. 'Sure, why not?'

He turned to his companions.

'We ain't got any objection to a little stroll to meet the marshal, have we boys?'

The others grinned.

'Sure, we're law-abidin' citizens.'

'Don't make any false moves,' Carson snapped.

He nodded in the direction of the

door, keeping his eye all the time on the gunslick's eyes, watching for that all but imperceptible flicker that could signal gunplay. The man shuffled forward a mere fraction, his right hand hovering over his holster. At the same instant, the man to his right went for his gun. Almost instantaneously Carson's gun was in his hand and spitting lead. The man crumpled, his weapon only just out of its holster. Carson swivelled and fired again and at the same time saw another of the gunslicks topple backwards as Tombstone's gun belched flame. The next instant he went down on one knee, firing at the ringleader and seeing him stagger backwards, blood oozing from a wound in his side. Tombstone had hurled himself sideways, fanning as he did so. Something tore into Carson's chest but he kept on firing. The smell of gun smoke hung heavy in the air as it billowed through the saloon. People were hiding behind tables or had thrown themselves to the floor. The glass at the back of the counter shattered into a thousand fragments and the whine of ricochets rang out. Another bullet struck Carson in the arm and his six-gun fell to the floor. A gunman stood over him with his revolver pointed at his head and the next instant the man's face exploded as Tombstone's bullet smashed into it. Carson saw a pool of blood running over the floor but could not tell whether it was his or someone else's. The sudden silence after the roar of the guns was almost palpable. The whole affair had lasted only a matter of seconds. The six gunslicks lay sprawled about the floor in a variety of twisted attitudes. Carson became aware of an intense pain in his chest and his left arm hung uselessly. Suddenly Tombstone was at his side.

'Can you move?' he said.

Carson nodded. Somehow, with Tombstone's help, he managed to find his feet. The saloon was just coming back to life as people emerged from their hiding places. Tombstone was helping Carson to the door and nobody made any attempt to stop them.

'Best thing we can do is get out of here quick,' Tombstone said.

They staggered through the batwing doors and made for their horses at the hitch rail. There was a shout from down the street and Carson saw the marshal running in their direction. With Tombstone's aid, he hoisted himself into the saddle and then they were off as a couple of shots rang out.

'Make for the ranch!' Tombstone yelled.

* * *

Their horses were not fully rested after their day in the hills but still made good ground. Carson was holding the reins in one hand. Blood was oozing from the wound to his chest and his head was pounding along with the rhythm of the horses' hoofs. Tombstone was leaning out and looking behind for signs of pursuit but they had a decent start on the marshal or anyone else. The pounding in Carson's head got worse and he was afraid he might faint. The miles passed. The horses were flagging. Foam flew from their mouths and their breathing was coming in heavy gasps but they were getting near to the Bar X. Soon the shadow of the ranch house loomed up and, driving their horses to a final effort, they galloped into the yard. The door to the bunkhouse flew open.

'Somebody lend a hand!' Tombstone shouted.

Routledge appeared on the veranda, followed by his daughter. She let out a gasp and sprang down the steps ahead of her father.

'Oh goodness!' she shouted. 'Is he hurt?'

Carson had slipped from the saddle and Tombstone was holding on to him. One of the ranch hands ran up and together they lifted him from the Appaloosa.

'Take him into the ranch house,'

Routledge snapped.

They carried Carson up the steps. Laura opened a door to a bedroom and they laid him gently on the bed.

'What happened?' Routledge said.

'Never mind that now,' she responded. 'Can't you see he's been wounded?'

She was agitated and upset but she had enough of her wits about her to begin to attend to the stricken man. Blackness had descended upon Carson but now he came round and began to look about him uncomprehendingly. Gathering his wits, he sought to reassure them.

'I'll be OK. They're both flesh wounds.'

He saw the anxious face of Laura bending over him and then he passed out once more.

When he came round it was to find his chest swathed in bandages and his arm in a sling. He felt weak and his chest hurt. For a few moments he didn't know where he was or what had happened. He strove to sit up but he was too feeble and it made his head throb. He was lying in a comfortable bed and he could see that the room was tastefully decorated in a feminine way. Chintz curtains hung at the window and there were flowers in vases. Turning his head, he could see a dressing table with a mirror on which stood various toiletries. A fragrant smell lingered in the air. As he took this in, the door opened and Laura appeared, carrying a tray.

'So you're awake,' she said. 'Good. I've made some broth for you.'

A memory stirred in Carson's brain: the oldster, Pack Rat Dan, had done the same.

She placed the tray on a small bedside table and sat on the edge of the bed. Carson attempted to sit up again but with similar results to the previous time.

'Here, let me help you,' Laura said.

With her assistance he succeeded in sitting up a little. She fluffed up the pillow and, spooning some broth, held it to his lips.

'I feel like I've been tromped by a mustang,' he said. 'Who bandaged me up?'

'The doctor. I changed the dressings.'

'I don't remember a thing about it.'

'Just as well. He'll be back to see you, but right now you've just got to rest.'

'What about Tombstone?' Carson said.

'Tombstone's fine. He told us about the fire at the line cabin and everything.'

Suddenly she seemed to choke.

'You're so stupid,' she said. 'How could the two of you have been so foolish as to take on those men? You know the marshal's been here?'

'The marshal! What did he want?'

'He wanted you. Father wouldn't allow him or his deputy in the house. Things got quite awkward but Father wouldn't give way. In the end, he rode back to town.'

'He might come back. I can't let you and your father be dragged into this. If you'll just help me get up.'

He struggled but it was no use. He was too weak. Gently, Laura eased him down again.

'You're not going anywhere,' she said. 'Besides, Father has his own reasons for not doing anything to help the marshal. Try not to get agitated.'

Gathering up the bowl and tray, she smiled at Carson and softly left the room.

A few minutes later the door opened once more and, looking up, Carson saw Tombstone's grizzled countenance.

'Howdy,' he said. 'Looks like you'll go to any lengths for an easy berth.'

Carson grinned. 'We sure taught those varmints a lesson,' he said.

'We sure did. I ain't had so much fun in a long time.'

Carson started to laugh and winced as pain shot through his chest once more.

'Easy pardner,' Tombstone said.

'I guess you'll be missin' the line shack,' Carson said.

'Sure am. Havin' to bed down with

the rest of the boys in the bunkhouse, but it ain't so bad. Still, I can't figure why those *hombres* decided to burn me out. I guess they're just tightenin' the screws on Mr Routledge.'

'Yeah, but I figure it's more personal.'

'Personal?' Tombstone replied. 'How do you mean?'

'I figure those *hombres* knew I'd been at the line cabin. It all ties in with the incident at the Bird Cage. They were tryin' to warn me off. If the message got through to Routledge as well, so much the better. And that means that Wesley Roach has got to be behind it.'

Tombstone was thoughtful. 'I see what you mean,' he said. 'But right now you need to do like Miss Laura tells you and get better.'

'Is this her room?' Carson said.

'Yup.'

'Where is she sleeping?'

'She ain't had any time for that, but there's a spare room nobody uses.'

'I feel bad about it,' Carson said. 'I

don't like causin' all this trouble'

Tombstone left the room and when Laura returned shortly afterwards Carson was asleep.

$$\star \quad \star \quad \star$$

Days passed. Laura kept a close watch on Carson, changed his dressings and prepared food. The doctor came out once more to check on his progress, and Tombstone paid him regular visits. Caleb Routledge also poked his head round the door, but he saw nothing of Rik. He was too busy supervising the roundup and the branding prior to moving the herd to the railhead. Carson was determined to get back on his feet for the drive. Although the wound to his chest had caused most concern, it was the damage to his left arm which worried him now. The bone had been chipped just above the elbow. At least it hadn't been badly smashed.

$$\star \quad \star \quad \star$$

It was afternoon. Caleb Routledge leaned against the corral rail talking with his son Rik and the two other ranchers who had pooled their herds for the cattle drive. The cattle had been gathered together and brought into the corrals where they had been left for a few days without food or water to tame them down. Routledge was looking at the bills of sale. Rik was anxious. The bank was applying pressure and without the money from the drive they would all go under. Rik cast his eye over the cattle.

'We'll have 'em trail-branded soon,' he said, 'and then I aim to get 'em movin' just as soon as the new grass comes up.'

'Sure. If we get them quickly to market we can rest them on the pastures for a spell before selling them.'

Routledge gave Rik a long hard look.

'You look tired, son,' he said. 'Don't go overdoing things.'

The two ranchers moved off and Rik was about to depart when suddenly

Tombstone came galloping into the yard.

'What is it?' Rik snapped.

'Marshal's comin' this way and he's got a bunch of riders with him.'

Routledge cursed under his breath. 'I thought we'd got away with things a bit easy. I bin half expectin' another visit.'

'Looks to me like they mean business this time,' Tombstone said. 'I figure it's maybe time Carson and me lit a shuck outa here.'

They ran into the ranch house. Carson was standing beside the bed. He had his clothes on and was just fastening on his gunbelt. He looked pale and drawn but his wounds were well on the way to healing.

'Figure I'm just about fit again,' he said.

'Just as well,' Tombstone replied. 'The marshal's on his way with a posse. I figure we need to make ourselves scarce.'

Just then Laura burst into the room. 'What are you doing out of bed?' she exclaimed when she saw Carson. Quickly Routledge explained the new situation to her.

'He's not fit,' she said.

'There's no time for this now,' Routledge snapped. 'I agree with Tombstone. I've already ordered your horses to be saddled. There are supplies in the saddle-bags. Now get out of here! I'll deal with the marshal.'

Carson was still feeling weak but as soon as he was in the saddle he felt better. The Appaloosa was an old friend. Tombstone was up on the skewbald. A little crowd had gathered in the yard, foremost among them being Laura. Carson couldn't be sure, but there seemed to be tears in her eyes.

'Please be careful!' she called.

They hadn't been gone long when the marshal and his posse arrived. Routledge waited in the ranch house affecting not to be aware of them coming. A voice rang out in the yard.

'Routledge! Come out here!'

Rik was looking out the window.

'Ten of 'em,' he said. 'Quite a big bunch to pick up two men.'

'Maybe they were expectin' some difficulties,' Routledge replied.

Again the voice boomed out. 'Routledge, git yourself out here! You got business with the law.'

Slowly Routledge made his way to the door, opened it and stepped out on to the veranda, flanked by his son.

'Well if it ain't the marshal,' he said. 'Haven't you got a job to do in town?'

'This is my job,' the marshal said.

'Are you sure? Seems to me you're on private property.'

'Never mind that,' the marshal snapped. 'I reckon you can guess what I'm doin' here.' He tapped his shirt pocket. 'I got all the authorization I need right here,' he said, 'to arrest that murderin' no-good drifter you bin shelterin'.'

'And who might that be?'

'You know who I mean. And while I'm at it, I'll have your friend — what's his name — Tombstone Smith. Here, take a look at these if you want.'

He threw the papers on the veranda. Routledge glanced in their direction but made no move to pick them up. He was taking a close look at the posse. They seemed to be as mean, hard-looking and ornery a bunch as he had clapped eyes on. One thing was for certain. They were not the ordinary citizens who might be expected to constitute such a group.

'I think this has gone far enough,' Routledge said. 'If you don't mind, I've got things to do and I'd appreciate it if you gentlemen would just turn right round and ride back where you came from.'

The marshal glanced at some of the others.

'Sorry, can't do that,' he said. 'Not until you hand over Carson.'

Turning to his neighbour he whispered something and the man laughed as he pulled another piece of paper from his jacket pocket. He handed it to the marshal who proceeded to unroll it.

'Take a look at this,' he said and held it up. It was a Wanted poster with the faces of Carson and Tombstone printed on it.

'They're wanted men, Routledge. If you refuse to cooperate, you'll be obstructin' the course of the law.'

Suddenly there was a movement behind Routledge and Laura appeared in the doorway. She came forward and stood by her father, taking his arm.

'I'll say it one more time,' the marshal said. 'Hand over Carson and Tombstone. I don't want any trouble. I'm here as a representative of the law.'

Routledge grimaced. 'Marshal Gillespie would never have acted in this way. You're not fit to fill his boots.'

'That's beside the point, Routledge.'

Routledge turned to his daughter. 'Go and ask Mr Carson to step out here,' he said.

A few minutes passed. Routledge could see that some of the posse were getting restless. One man's hand hung menacingly over his six-gun.

'Why's she takin' so long?'

'You may remember,' Routledge replied, 'that Mr Carson is carrying some injuries. It may take a little time for him to comply.'

'Let's just go in and take him,' the man fingering his gun said.

'If necessary,' the marshal replied.

At that point Laura appeared again in the doorframe looking startled.

'What is it?' Routledge said.

'Mr Carson! He's gone!'

The marshal jumped down from his horse and without asking strode into the ranch house. Routledge made no attempt to stop him but simply followed.

'He was in this room,' he said, showing the marshal into Laura's bedroom. The window stood open and a thin curtain was flapping in the breeze.

'He can't have got far!' the marshal snapped. He turned to Routledge. 'Did you know anything about this?'

Routledge expressed his innocence.

Anger spread across the marshal's face but he managed to calm down. 'Never mind,' he said. 'I'll get back to you later.'

Turning on his heels, he stamped out of the room, pushing Rik aside in his haste. As he mounted his horse, young Lou Reynolds burst out of the bunkhouse.

'No sign of Tombstone,' he called. 'Must be out on the range.'

The marshal wheeled his horse. 'You'd better hope we find them,' he flung back over his shoulder. Followed by the posse, he rode out of the yard.

'Well,' said Routledge, turning to his daughter, 'they seem to be an unhappy crew.'

Laura seemed to be unsure whether to laugh or to cry.

'We haven't heard the last of this,' Rik said. 'I hope we know what we're doin'.'

5

A meeting was taking place in Canyon Kate's office. Locked in discussion were Kate, Otis Griffin, Cobb and Wesley Roach.

'It'll be OK,' Kate was saying. 'You've got yourself all riled up about nothing.'

'I just don't like it, Ma,' Roach said. 'Who is this guy Carson? Why is he askin' questions?'

'He's one man. What harm can he possibly do you?'

'You shouldn't have let him get away. I'm gonna have to do somethin' about Cindy.'

'It wasn't her fault. Carson must have heard the boys comin' up the stairs.' Annoyance was written across Griffin's face.

'You're all incompetent,' he shouted. 'Cobb, what sort of idiot are you? You had Carson behind bars and you let

99

him walk. And now you've let him escape again. Why do you think I put you in office? You'd better not let me down another time.'

'Calm down,' Kate intervened.

'When I moved your son and his gunslick friends on to the Slash H, I expected them to have dealt with Routledge by now. All they've done is steal a few head of cattle. I could have got my own boys to do that.'

Canyon Kate sidled up to Griffin and put her head on his shoulder but he shook her off.

'Listen carefully,' Griffin fumed. 'I want this Carson hombre found and put out of circulation. After that you can deal with Routledge.'

'Don't worry yourself none,' Roach replied. 'Me an' the boys will take care of things.'

Kate looked at her son. There was a glint in his eye.

'Just make sure you do it,' Griffin said.

There was silence for a few moments

and then Roach, striking his knee with his hand, burst into laughter.

'What's the joke?' Griffin barked.

'I think I just worked out how to get Carson.'

'Let's hear it.'

'Well, seems to me what we need is something to lure him down from those hills or wherever he's hidin'. Now just think, what's it goin' to take?'

Kate looked thoughtful. 'Now, you wouldn't be thinkin' of a certain rancher's lovely daughter?' she said.

Roach leered at his mother.

'Miss Laura Routledge,' she continued. 'Am I right?'

'Yeah, Miss Laura. After all, it was Carson came to her rescue after we skittered her horse and buggy. I'd be willin' to bet she's been lookin' after him since he got shot. I figure that if somethin' was to happen to Laura Routledge he'd pretty soon come ridin' down outa those hills. Like maybe a kidnappin', for instance. She spends a lot of time ridin' about on her own.'

'Good idea,' the marshal said. 'It could take time to flush Carson out. This way we could have him just where we want him.'

Griffin rose, dusted his sharp black suit and placed his hat on his head.

'Just do whatever it takes,' he said. 'And don't let me have to be bothered with any more of this.'

He turned to Canyon Kate. 'Keep your son in order. I would hate to see you lose the Bird Cage.'

He opened the door and slammed his way along the corridor and down the stairs.

Marshal Cobb followed him. When they had gone, Wesley Roach turned to his mother.

'I could do with a little relaxation,' he said. 'Where's Cindy?'

'She's not got a client. I'll send her to you. And maybe one or two of the other girls just to help along?'

Downstairs the piano began to play.

★ ★ ★

When Carson and Tombstone galloped out of the Bar X ranch they headed towards the foothills, passing the burned-out ruins of the line cabin on their way. Occasionally they looked behind them but there were no signs of pursuit. They rode up the slopes until they saw a patch of scrub oak where they brought their horses to a halt. From their place of concealment they had a good view over the valley. Carson reached for his field glasses but he had left them behind.

'Damn!' he said. 'They would have been real useful.'

'Sure would,' Tombstone grinned. 'That's why I brought this.' He felt behind his blanket roll and came up with an instrument in leather wrapping which he handed to Carson. It was a spyglass, about nine inches long with an orange-stained body tube and tooled decorations and was signed *Leonardo Semitecolo Venezia.*

'Eighteenth century,' Tombstone said. 'Take a look through it.'

Carson surveyed the scene.

'Kinda goes with the eye patch, don't you think?' Tombstone said.

'Did this come from one of your catalogues?'

'In a way,' Tombstone replied. 'It's one of the few things didn't get burned up in that fire. Thing is, now you've had a chance to look around, what have you come up with?'

'Listen,' said Carson. 'If you were the marshal where would you expect us to be headin'.'

'Right where we are,' Tombstone said.

'Exactly. They'll be expectin' us to head for the mountains. But how about if we try the unexpected.'

'I see what you're drivin' at. The posse will come this way. It's only natural. So where do you reckon we should go?'

'You know this country better than I do. What do you think?'

Tombstone looked away across the valley. As far as the eye could see stretched the rolling pasture lands.

'South,' he said. 'Keep ridin' and you reach the Big Ooze. Beyond that there's nothin' much. Most of it is Injun country. They call it the Wastelands. A man could be sort of exposed but on the other hand he could get lost. 'Specially if no one reckoned to find him there.'

'How far to the Big Ooze?'

'Two, three days maybe? It's a long time since I bin that way.'

'OK. Let's ride south.'

Tombstone spat a jet of liquid from between his two exposed front teeth. 'How long do you aim to keep ridin'?' he asked. 'Beyond the Big Ooze?'

Carson grinned. 'Just as long as it takes the marshal and his boys to get tired of lookin' for us up here.'

Getting back into the saddle, they rode down from the foothills.

★　★　★

It was after they had been riding for two days that Carson saw the first sign

105

of a cattle trail. It came in from the north and east and it was faint, as if small numbers of cows had passed that way. There was not much left of their tracks but there were tell-tale droppings.

'Interestin',' Tombstone commented. 'Now who do you think would want to trail cattle down thisaway?'

'I think we can make a pretty good guess,' Carson answered. 'No wonder we didn't find anythin' up in the hills.'

Riding a little further, they reached a small creek whose banks had been partly trampled down. They discovered some cow tracks with possible impressions of earlier crossings. And now and again there were vague, faded hoof prints.

'Yup,' Carson said. 'I figure we've solved the mystery of what happened to those missin' cattle.'

'Not too far to the Big Ooze,' Tombstone said. 'What's the bettin' we'll find them cow critters somewhere on the other side?'

'If so,' Carson said, 'we'd better take care. There'll probably be some of Griffin's men left behind to keep an eye on things.'

Later, Carson's suspicions were confirmed when they came upon the remains of a camp. It looked to Tombstone as if three men had been in camp and they'd maybe had pack horses.

'Supplies,' Carson said. 'Looks like they got a real operation goin' on. A neat set-up. Take a few cows each time and faze 'em on down to the Big Ooze. Anyone gettin' suspicious would just naturally expect them to be hidden in the hills.'

'Yeah, we made that mistake. Cost us a day's ridin'.'

'And don't forget the line cabin. Mighta been a different story if we'd been around.'

They reached the Big Ooze, splashing their horses through the shallow water. At no point did it rise higher than their horses' bellies. There were some indications that cattle had been moved across and, riding up to some higher ground to take a look through Tombstone's spyglass, Carson could see further down what looked like a trail leading into and out of the water. Turning in that direction, they rode till they were among the trees and then they dropped from the saddle. Tying their horses, they went forward on foot. When they calculated to have almost reached the spot Tombstone held up his hand.

'Listen!' he whispered.

A rising breeze was blowing through the trees and on it they could hear faint sounds of lowing cattle.

'Let's take a closer look,' Carson said.

They found the cattle on a broad patch of level ground, lying down and chewing the cud, and when they examined the brands their suspicions were finally confirmed. Most bore the Bar X brand but there was also Rafter and Anvil Bar stock.

'So they ain't got round to re-brandin' 'em yet,' Tombstone said. 'They certainly don't seem to be bothered about anyone findin' 'em out.'

'Why should they?' Carson replied. 'Griffin's got the law in his pocket.'

Returning to their horses, they found somewhere to camp. After staking the horses out to graze, they worked on building a fire as rain began to spatter.

'Hell,' Carson said. 'What are we doin' here?'

'Hidin',' Tombstone replied. 'And if we hadn't of rode here we wouldn't have found the cattle.'

'Yeah, there's that to be said. But so far it's bin Griffin runnin' the show from rustlin' the cattle to burnin' down the line cabin and forcin' us on the lam.'

'Don't take it amiss. I know you got shot an' all,' Tombstone said, 'but I sure enjoyed takin' it to those varmints in the saloon.'

'Yeah, me too. Apart from gettin' shot, that is.'

They both laughed.

'Make sure it don't happen that way next time,' Tombstone said.

'That's it,' Carson said. 'I'm plumb sick of bein' on the receivin' end. I think it's about time we took it to Griffin.'

They were both quiet. The shadows of the firelight flickered among the trees.

'What you got in mind?' Tombstone said.

'I ain't too sure. You're the one who's done the readin'. What do you reckon those books of yours might suggest?'

Tombstone grinned. 'How about we become temporary members of Griffin's bunch of gunslicks?'

Carson gave him a puzzled look.

'Look,' Tombstone continued. 'We know the rustled cows are here. There's got to be a few of Griffin's men keepin' a loose eye on 'em. How long they been doin' that? Long enough not to know much about what's bin happenin' back at the Slash H. OK. What's to stop us ridin' in on whoever's takin' care of things here on the Big Ooze? They don't know nothin' about us. That way we'd be on the inside. We might get the

110

low-down on Griffin once an' for all. Roach, too, if he's involved.'

Carson was thinking. 'And what happens then?' he said. 'Somebody would soon recognize us.'

'OK, there's a weak link,' Tombstone said. 'I ain't just thought it out that far.'

Carson whistled softly. 'You know, you might be on to somethin'.'

'You ever hear the story of the wooden horse?' Tombstone asked.

'Nope, but I reckon I might of rode him a time or two,' Carson replied.

'It was round the time of the battle of Troy.'

'I bin there too,' Carson said. 'Back east, a long time ago. Stopped there on my way to Buffalo. Didn't know there'd been a battle, though.'

'Remind me to tell you about it sometime,' Tombstone said.

★ ★ ★

Back at the Bar X, Routledge was worrying about his daughter. She had

111

gone riding on her favourite horse, a chestnut gelding she called Blue. Normally there would be no need for concern but things were different since Griffin and his hardcases had entered the scene. Was there anything more to the episode of the runaway horse and buggy? It was lucky Carson had been on hand. She hadn't been gone too long but her father was already listening for the sound of her horse's hoofs in the yard.

Laura had set off with the intention of riding into town. There were a couple of items she wanted at the general store but that was not the main reason for her choice of direction. Maybe she would be able to pick up some information about what had happened to Carson and Tombstone. Really, she just wanted to be doing something, to be somewhere she might hear a mention of Carson's name. However, it was a beautiful day and she did not take the trail for town but headed off across the rangeland, letting her horse have its head. It was a good cutting horse and trained to go from a standing start into a quick burst of speed. The ride was exhilarating but it was brought to a sudden halt.

From out of nowhere Laura heard the sharp *thwack* of something flying overhead and she realized it was a bullet. Pulling on the reins she turned the gelding in a different direction. The horse was running fast when a second shot rang out and this time the horse went plunging head foremost, shot through the neck, and flinging Laura from the saddle. Laura hit the ground hard and for a moment or two she was winded. Struggling to her knees she looked up as two riders galloped up to her. One of them was carrying a rifle. They were thin, wiry and dirty looking. The one without the rifle was chewing a wad of tobacco.

'Nice shootin',' he said to his companion and they both laughed as they dismounted.

Laura struggled to her feet. 'Blue!' she cried.

Ignoring the two men she ran up to the horse but it was clear that it was dead. She turned back to the two riders. 'You've killed my horse!' she shouted. 'You've killed my horse!'

Overcome with grief and anger she rushed upon them. She was sobbing uncontrollably and struck out at them with her fists. The men laughed again; one of them got behind her, pinioning her arms and restraining her. Still she struggled and then the other one hit her hard across the face with the flat of his hand.

'Take it easy, lady!' he hissed.

'My horse! Blue!' she shouted. 'You didn't have to kill my horse!'

The man struck her again and blood ran down from her nose and lip. She stopped struggling and would have sunk to the ground had her assailant not prevented it.

'That's better,' the other one said.

'Let's get her up on your horse,' his

companion said.

They seized her as she dragged her feet but she was helpless to resist her attackers. Between them they pulled and pushed her up on one of the horses.

'What do you think you're doing?' she asked.

'Just takin' you for a little ride.'

'Who are you? What are you doing on Bar X property?'

They had swung themselves up into leather and now they started to ride at a steady jog. The man behind her smelled bad and his breath was rancid. Not turning round, she shouted: 'Where are you taking me? Let me go. Now!'

'Like I say, just a little ride, lady.'

She saw that it was pointless to ask questions that might only rile them further. They had already shown how little respect she could expect from them and for the first time she began to fear for what they might do to her. Who were they? She wasn't sure in which direction they were heading. At first it seemed they might be going towards the Slash H and she felt a brief surge of hope. She had no liking for Griffin but he seemed to represent a better prospect than the other possible options. Then she realized they were riding away from the hills and her heart sank. She guessed that they were heading south towards the Big Ooze, an area which people had so far tended to avoid. Beyond that lay rough country and the Indian territories. She was very afraid.

6

Riding deeper into Big Ooze country Carson and Tombstone found other cattle grazing in small groups or singly. Most of them wore the Bar X brand. The grass was thinner down here. Clouds of black flies hovered in the air. Presently they saw a thin line of smoke.

'Range brandin',' Tombstone said.

'Remember your lines,' Carson replied and they both grinned.

Ahead of them they could see a group of men and cattle. One man on horseback cast his rope over the head of a calf which he then dragged towards the fire.

'Calf on the ground!'

So far, none of the rustlers had observed their approach through the smoky, dusty air. The calf was wriggling and bawling.

'Hot iron!'

'What do you bet?' Carson said.

'Slash H,' Tombstone replied.

Wailing dolefully, the released calf struggled to its feet and went off seeking its mother. The men looked up. There were six of them in all, five working round the fire and the one on horseback who pulled a rifle out of its scabbard.

'Glad we found you boys!' Carson called.

They rode slowly up and halted. Carson suddenly felt conspicuous. For a few moments there was silence. The man with the branding iron had dropped it to the ground and now he stepped forward.

'Who the hell are you?' he said.

'Hey, no need to get suspicious. Why doesn't he just put down that rifle?'

'Not till we know who you are. And your story had better be good.'

'We're ridin' for the same brand,' Carson replied. 'Mr Griffin sends his regards.'

'Griffin? He didn't say nothin' about sendin' more men.'

Carson had a sudden inspiration. 'Roach had a word with him. He figures you boys might be gettin' a bit restless. Could maybe do with a night or two in town. We're here as replacements.'

'Don't sound right to me,' someone piped up. 'It ain't like Roach to take an interest in what happens to the rest of us.'

'Maybe he's gettin' mellow,' Carson said. 'Spendin' time at that old Bird Cage is makin' him soft.'

Mention of the Bird Cage brought a chuckle from some of the rustlers.

'I ain't sayin' no to a chance of gettin' out of here for awhiles,' another man said.

'What we got to lose. There's only the two of 'em.'

'We can turn right round if that's what you want,' Carson said.

The man with the branding iron came to a decision.

'We're about finished here,' he said. 'Saddle up and we'll head back to the cabin. Let Carlyon decide.'

He picked up the iron and carried it back to the fire. One of the men grabbed a coffee pot and hurled its contents on the flames. The others stamped it out. Mounting their horses which were tethered nearby, they set off with Carson and Tombstone.

'Funny,' the nearest one said, 'I ain't seen either of you two before.'

'We only hit town last week.'

'Is that so? You friends of Roach?'

Carson was aware he needed to speak and act carefully. 'You could say that,' he said.

Suddenly the man's face brightened. 'Hey, you two wouldn't be the same *hombres* Roach was ridin' with up around Silver Junction?'

Carson nodded. 'We bin up around those parts,' he said.

The man grinned. 'Boy!' he said. 'I got to hand it to you.'

He turned in the saddle to face Carson. 'You still got your share of that gold?'

'Maybe,' Carson said.

'That old man sure did Roach a favour. Had himself the time of his life blowin' the loot. He showed us the old timer's scalp. I ain't laughed so much in a long time. He musta looked a rare sight, completely bald an' all.'

Carson felt a surge of anger but kept it concealed.

'You got to hand it to Roach,' the man said. 'He don't care at all, just does whatever it takes.'

They continued to ride, not saying anything. Tombstone had overheard some of the conversation and gave Carson a questioning look. Carson's ploy had worked. There was no doubt now that Roach was in with Griffin. Carson felt that he was getting close to nailing the old man's killer.

When they arrived at their destination it was to find that it was rather more than a cabin. In fact, it was quite an imposing cluster of buildings composing a basic ranch house with outbuildings and corrals, one of which contained horses. As they approached, the door of the main building opened and a man stepped forward. He was heavily built and had closely cropped hair.

'We got company. Figured we'd best bring 'em in, Carlyon.'

Carlyon turned to a man who had just emerged through the door.

'Take their horses,' he said.

He directed his attention to Carson.

'We don't get a lot of visitors,' he said.

'We ain't visitors. Griffin sent us over.'

'Why should I believe that?'

'He's not lyin',' the man Carson had been talking to cut in. 'He rode with Roach up around Silver Junction.'

Carlyon eyed Carson closely.

'That apply to your friend too?'

Carson nodded. A slow smile spread across Carlyon's features.

'You'd better come inside,' he said, 'and get acquainted.'

As soon as he did, Carson knew that something was wrong, something which threatened the whole charade. Lying on a chair was a hat, a woman's hat which Carson recognized. It was Laura's! What was it doing here? What had happened to her? If Laura was somewhere around she would recognize him and give the game away. His eyes flickered around the room. It was sparsely furnished and there was a door at the back opening on to another room. Could she be in there?

'So you're new to these parts?' Carlyon said.

'Only got into town recently,' Carson replied.

Carlyon turned his attention to Tombstone. 'He don't say much,' he said.

'Nope. I guess you could say he's the quiet type.'

Carlyon looked long and hard at Tombstone. Finally he spoke to Carson once more.

'Git your stuff from the stables,' he said. 'You can sleep in the barn. Supper's at eight. Tomorrow we start at sunup.'

He didn't say what they would be

starting and Carson didn't stop to ask him. Together he and Tombstone made their way to the stables where their horses had been groomed and fed. Taking some items from their saddle-bags they made their way out of the door and across the yard to the barn. There was a pile of hay stacked in one corner.

'Guess he meant here,' Tombstone said.

'Be quiet,' Carson answered. 'You talk too much.'

They threw their things down.

'You saw the hat?' Carson said.

'I saw it,' Tombstone replied. 'Now what do you suppose a lady's hat is doin' here?'

'Not just any lady's hat,' Carson replied. 'That hat belongs to Miss Laura.'

'Miss Laura!'

'She wears it when she goes out ridin'.'

They looked at each other.

'D'you think some of Griffin's boys

maybe come across her when she was ridin' and kidnapped her?' Tombstone said.

'Looks that way.'

'Then they must have brought her here. She must be somewhere around.'

'There was a door leading out of the room they took us in. Maybe she's in there?'

'Wherever she is, she can't be far away.'

'What do you propose doin'?' Tombstone said.

'We don't want to arouse any suspicions. I reckon that Carlyon hombre has his doubts already. We'll get along to the bunkhouse when it's supper time. Act normal. When it's dark we'll do a bit of snooping.'

Tombstone nodded. 'Why do you think they would kidnap her?'

'Who knows? Maybe Griffin sanctioned it. Maybe a couple of his gunslicks just took matters into their own hands.' Carson paused, thinking. 'Or maybe it's some ploy to bring us out into the open. Me in particular.'

'You could be right. Marshal Cobb wouldn't relish ridin' about with that posse for too long.'

'Especially if he was under pressure. All along, they seem to have been a mite jumpy at the mention of Wesley Roach. They would know that I wouldn't be likely to hear about Miss Laura's disappearance without tryin' to do somethin' about it. But what I can't quite figure is how they would expect me to know about it.'

'It wouldn't be hard,' Tombstone said. 'News gets around mighty fast. Especially about somethin' like that. We'd have got to hear about it one way and another.'

'It adds up,' Carson concluded.

Eight o'clock arrived and they made their way to what passed as the bunkhouse. The rustlers they had met range branding were all there together with Carlyon and the other man from the ranch house. In addition there were a couple of newcomers. They were grimy and covered with dust, having ridden in not long before. Carson was taking notice of their numbers. Maybe there were others either here or out on the range. It added up to a decent complement. Taken with the buildings and the corrals, it amounted to quite a going concern. Carson was worried about what questions they might be asked but the meal was remarkably silent. He had never come across a more unpleasant-looking crew. They wore their guns at table and certainly weren't regular cow punchers. So what were they doing guarding cattle in this god-forsaken spot? Obviously Griffin must be paying them well but they could hardly be happy with the situation. If it came to the push, how loyal to Griffin were they likely to be? Or was their loyalty more to Wesley Roach? A lot of questions were arising in Carson's mind, not least among them why Carlyon, who was obviously in charge, seemed uninterested in finding out more about them. He decided it was because it made no difference. He had already decided that they were dead men. In which case, their time was strictly limited and they needed to act real quick.

★   ★   ★

Back at the Bar X, the first reaction when Laura failed to return was to organize a search, and it didn't take Rik long to find the dead horse. He was no expert in reading sign but there was still a faded trail leading in the direction of the Slash H. He rode that way but after a time he lost it and headed instead for the Bar X. His father had ridden with a few of the hands in the direction of the north range and the burned-out line cabin but it wasn't long before they came riding back, arriving not long after Rik. Quickly he told them what he had found.

'You say the trail led towards the Slash H!' his father exclaimed. 'OK, let's ride.'

'The trail petered out,' Rik said. 'There's nothing to say the Slash H has to be involved.'

'Someone shot your sister's horse and took her!' his father shouted. 'Who else do you suggest?'

'It could have been anybody.'

'Well, I ain't stickin' around to find out. Come on, boys, let's not waste time.'

There was a clattering of hoofs in the yard. Reluctantly, Rik followed. He was as angry as the next man but he was attempting to think the thing through in a sensible way. To be honest, he also felt a vague sense of anger and frustration at his sister. Time after time she had been warned against her headstrong ways by both her father and himself. She was irresponsible. Right now, he was worn down with worries about the forthcoming cattle drive, the outcome of which was make or break. He could ill afford this latest distraction.

Before they ever reached the Slash H spread they were intercepted by a bunch of Griffin's hardcases who came riding down on them from two different directions. Routledge drew his men to a halt.

'Hold it right there!' the leader of the riders said.

Routledge recognized him as Mart Adams, a man who had been with Griffin before the arrival of the gunslicks who now seemed to be part of his main workforce.

'This is Slash H property. I think you'd better turn right round.'

'You know what we're here for,' Routledge said. 'What have you done with her?'

'Done with who? What do you mean?'

'Don't give me that,' Routledge said. 'You know what I mean. What have you done with my daughter?'

Adams was genuinely puzzled, and Rik realized that this was probably because the abduction had taken place only hours before. He stepped his horse forward.

'Miss Routledge went riding earlier

today,' he said. 'She didn't come back. I found her horse. It had been shot and there was no sign of her.'

'So you come ridin' in here like a bunch of roustabouts at trail's end,' Adams replied. 'What makes you think anybody here knows about it?'

Rik was silent.

'You got some of your gunslicks ridin' right there with you,' Routledge said. 'Why don't you try askin' some of them?'

One of them rode forward.

'Stay outa this!' Adams said.

'Stay outa nothin',' the man replied.

He turned to Routledge. 'Seems to me you're makin' accusations without a lot of proof. Like the man said, you better turn round and git back where you came from.'

'I ain't goin' nowhere. And you ain't stoppin' us ridin' right up to the Slash H to see for ourselves whether you got my daughter.'

He spurred his horse but the other man barred his way. Two more riders came into view. It was Griffin and Marshal Cobb.

'Now what seems to be the problem?' Cobb said as he came alongside.

'Where have you got my daughter?' Routledge said, turning to Griffin.

'I don't know what this is all about,' Griffin said, 'but whatever the disagreement, this is not the place to settle it.'

He turned to the Slash H riders. 'OK boys!' he shouted. 'You've done a good job but me and the marshal will take over from here. Get back to your work.'

There was still a lot of tension in the air and the hardcase who had ridden forward to challenge Routledge seemed particularly disgruntled. He looked hard at Routledge before spurring his horse away. The rest of the Slash H men turned their horses and started to ride.

'Thank you,' Griffin said to Adams. 'Make sure the boys do as they're told.'

Adams nodded and rode off.

'Now if you tell your men to do the same, perhaps we can discuss this matter back at my ranch. The marshal here will see to it that everything's fair and square.'

'You'd better have a good story,' Routledge said. 'Rik, come with me. The rest of you go back to the Bar X.'

There was a slight hesitation.

'Are you sure boss?' somebody called.

Routledge looked a lot less than satisfied with the way things had turned out but his initial burst of outrage had subsided and he could see that there was little he could do for the moment. If Griffin was involved, he might find evidence of Laura's whereabouts at the Slash H.

'You boys go back,' he said. 'For now.'

Rik was relieved. The situation for a time had looked ugly. The Bar X men had been outnumbered and most of Griffin's boys looked like they knew how to shoot. But he had a feeling that the respite was only temporary. While the others set off for the Bar X, he rode with his father to the Slash H.

After eating their meal, Carson and Tombstone took a slow, roundabout route back to the barn. The outbuildings were locked and nobody seemed to be about. Carson surreptitiously knocked on the doors but there was no response. When they came past the main building again they could hear talk and laughter.

'I reckon Laura is being held in that other room,' Carson said. 'I guess we just have to wait.'

The night wore on. Watching from the doorway of the barn, Carson saw the door of the ranch house open and three men come out. They made their way to the bunkhouse. Presently, a couple more emerged and he could see Carlyon standing in the doorway. One of the men shouted something and Carlyon laughed. Shortly after their departure the lights went out in the ranch house.

'I guess Carlyon is settlin' down in

there,' Carson said. 'But how many others are there?'

Tombstone shrugged.

'This is what we'll do,' Carson said. 'You get back to the barn. Be careful in case there's anyone still about. Get three horses saddled and ready. Wait behind the horse corral.'

'And what do you propose to do?'

'I aim to sneak in there while everyone's asleep.'

'Yeah? And then what?'

'Slip into the other room, wake Laura if she's sleeping too, and get her out.'

'Carson, I see you've been giving this plan a lot of thought just like the others. I reckon they should make you a perfessor.'

Carson chuckled. 'You're the one reads encyclopaedias,' he retorted. 'Have you got a better one?'

'Maybe about three or four steps back along the line. But right now I can't think of anythin' else. Leastways, only one small thing.'

'What's that?'

Tombstone dug in his pocket. 'You might need this again.'

It was the key they had used to break out of the jail.

'Maybe the door to the ranch house is open,' Tombstone said. 'Maybe the door to Laura's room is open — if she's there at all. You could be plumb lucky. But take it anyway.'

'You'd be better with the key,' Carson said.

'You take it. If Miss Laura is in there, she'll respond better to you puttin' in an appearance than an ornery old goat like me. When do we start?'

Carson took a final look outside. The whole place was in darkness. 'No time like the present. I'll give you a few minutes to make your way to the stables. Let's go.'

With a quick glance to left and right, Tombstone slipped through the barn door. He was soon swallowed up in shadows. Carson waited impatiently, ticking off the seconds. The night was silent except for the occasional snicker of a horse. At last, he slid from the barn and made his way silently across the short distance which separated him from the ranch house. Pressing himself against the wall, he listened intently for any sounds from within. He could hear nothing. Quickly but silently he reached the door and touched the handle, hoping that it might have been left unlocked; it was shut tight. Reaching into his shirt pocket he drew out Tombstone's key and was just about to insert it into the lock when his eye was attracted to a darker patch against the wall and he realized that one of the windows had been left slightly ajar. Putting the key back into his pocket he crept silently to the window and crouched beneath it, listening again for any sounds from within. Still he could hear nothing. Raising himself gently, he peered through the window. It was dark inside and at first his eyes could pick out nothing substantial but then he thought he could detect a dark shape slumped in one corner and another against the right-hand wall, which he guessed were the sleeping forms of Carlyon and one of his men. Suddenly there was a low grunt and one of the shapes seemed to move. Carson ducked down and waited for any repetition of the noise but whoever had stirred in his sleep appeared to have settled down again.

Getting to his feet, Carson placed his fingers beneath the window sash and with extreme care began to raise it, praying it would not creak. His hand was shaking; he wasn't sure whether it was with sheer tension or the weight of the sash, which was surprisingly heavy. He did not dare raise it very high — just till there was sufficient space for him to put his leg through. Feeling very carefully with his foot, he balanced the rest of his body on the window ledge and slithered silently into the darkened room. Fortunately it was only a small drop but his feet still made a slight noise as he landed. He did not move but remained crouching against the inside wall before creeping silently across the room to the door at the far end. Now was the most nerve-racking time of all. Listening again to the men breathing and feeling reasonably satisfied that they were undisturbed, he put his hand on the door handle. The door was locked. There was nothing to be done except put his hope and trust in Tombstone's skeleton key. With infinite care and patience he pushed it into the lock and tried to turn it. There was no response. He tried turning it the other way and there was a slight movement but still the door remained firmly locked. He was afraid to move the key about too much and it suddenly seemed a hopeless enterprise. Then he remembered that the key had served its purpose once before and again began to fumble at the locked door, pulling the key towards him and attempting to twist it as he did so. Suddenly there was a low click and something gave. Standing rigid against the door, Carson waited for any response to the slight noise but there was none.

Now Carson had to worry about who might be on the opposite side of the door. Would Laura be there? Would she be guarded? Pushing gently, Carson opened the door just sufficiently for him to slip through. Although his eyes had adjusted to the interior darkness, this room was even blacker than the other. There was no window to let in the merest hint of light. He could see very little, but his ears detected the clear sound of breathing. Someone was asleep in the room. Surely, it had to be Laura! Silently and stealthily he tiptoed forward, guided more by sound than by sight till his eyes could pick out the dark shape of a bedstead with a huddled figure lying upon it. Getting down on one knee, he peered closely, lifting the edge of a blanket to get a clearer impression. There was a smudged mass of hair which told him he had found the kidnapped girl. She was breathing heavily and he feared that she might have been drugged to keep her quiet when suddenly there was a flicker of movement and one eye opened. It looked blankly up at him. Clapping one hand across her mouth, he whispered as clearly but as unthreateningly as he could:

'Don't make any noise. It's me. Carson.'

There was a movement of her head under the blanket. Slowly he took his hand away from her mouth.

'What are you doing here?' she breathed.

'There's no time to ask questions. Just trust me. We've got to get away. There are two people sleeping in the next room. We must be very, very quiet. Can you get up without making any sound?'

In the darkness he could see her head nod. Then the blanket was moved aside and she swung her legs to the ground. As far as he could make out she was wearing her normal riding gear.

'Are you sure you're OK?' he whispered. 'You're not hurt at all?'

'I'm OK,' she said.

141

Silently they moved towards the door, Laura clinging to Carson's arm. In the room beyond they could see the partly opened window. Stealthily they crept towards it, listening closely for any indications of disturbance in the breathing patterns of the two sleeping gunmen. There was a faint noise as Laura's foot scuffed against a slightly raised portion of the packed earth floor and they froze as the man nearest the wall stirred. Hardly daring to breathe, they waited till he seemed to have settled again. They reached the window and Carson attempted to indicate by signs the best way for Laura to climb through. It was not high and she showed a natural agility as Carson assisted her to reach up. There was a brief hiatus and then the faintest of sounds from outside indicated that she had landed safely. It was Carson's turn now and it took him only a matter of seconds to climb through and join her. How good the night air felt on their faces. Not daring to speak, Carson indicated where they should go and they moved quickly and silently towards the stables. Keeping to the shelter of the stable wall, they made their way to the corral, which was situated in its rear. Some of the horses stirred at their approach. Carson's eyes were searching for Tombstone but there was no sign of him. While they waited, Carson took the opportunity to briefly explain Tombstone's role in the proceedings. Laura and Carson both peered into the darkness. There was a slight sound and Carson's hand went towards his gun but it was only Tombstone.

'This way,' he said. 'I had to move the horses back. Someone approached the stable. At first I thought it was you.'

'Quick,' Carson said, slightly alarmed at Tombstone's words. Things had gone well. He didn't want anything to foul it up now. Like phantoms, they ghosted through the shadows. The horses were standing in the shelter of some trees. Their ears were pricked and one of them whinnied at their approach. Laura turned to say something to Carson but he shook his head and ushered her forwards. The next moment they had swung into leather and were moving towards the open country which stretched dark and mysterious all around. It was difficult to determine directions but Carson calculated that the route they were following would lead them eventually to the Big Ooze.

After they had been riding for a while Carson drew his horse to a halt, the others following his example. He listened carefully. When he was satisfied that there were no sounds of pursuit he signalled for them to continue. Occasionally they could see big dim shapes which Carson took to be cattle but there were no signs of any human activity. On they went at a steady lope, and as they rode Carson tried to figure what their next move should be. If Laura's kidnap had been intended to flush them out into the open, it had worked. It wouldn't be hard for Roach or Griffin to realize what had happened. There was little doubt that they were in it together. But who was now the real power? Griffin had apparently called in Roach and his gunslicks to further his cause. But what was that old saying? If you sup with the devil, use a long spoon.

Suddenly his thoughts were interrupted by a call from Tombstone.

'Thought I heard something.'

Carson had been distracted; now he snapped to attention, peering into the blackness and holding up his hand as a signal for them to stop. They reined in the horses and listened closely.

'Riders!' he said.

Tombstone nodded. Carlyon and his men had awakened to their absence. They set off again, this time spurring their horses to a gallop. Laura was an accomplished horsewoman and easily kept pace with Carson and Tombstone as they thundered across the shadowy landscape. Carson peered round as they plunged on but night's dark blanket still concealed any sign of pursuit. He began to search for somewhere they might hide. The horses slowed as they crossed a narrow stream bed and then they could discern trees leading down to what was probably another creek.

'Make for the trees!' Carson shouted.

It seemed to Carson as good a spot as they were likely to find. Carlyon couldn't be certain in which direction they had gone. He had probably split his forces. That would even up the odds if it came to a showdown. They were riding down into the trees now. A pale glimmer of light indicated the presence of water, and walking their horses into the stream they followed it a little way till it began to widen and they halted in the shelter of the cottonwoods.

'This will have to do,' Carson said.

He guessed the stream was a tributary of the Big Ooze. They dismounted and then tethered their horses.

'Keep close behind us,' Carson said to Laura. 'And do whatever I ask.'

They slipped out of the sheltering trees and waded in the shallow waters of the stream. Moving up the river bank, they halted at last behind some trees which gave them a view of the surrounding country across which they had ridden. It was still very dark but dawn was approaching. Crouched in the shelter of the trees, Tombstone and Carson scanned the dimly veiled landscape and listened intently for the sound of horses' hoofs. It was not long till they heard them, still some distance away but bearing down remorselessly. Tombstone had his ear to the ground.

'I reckon four, maybe five.'

The sounds of pursuit were now unmistakable and soon Tombstone's keen eyes picked out something moving against the backcloth of night. Something gleamed for a moment — a reflection from a harness or the barrel of a rifle. The riders slowed and then stopped. There was a moment's pause and then they started up again, changing direction so that they were heading straight for the line of trees where their quarry lay concealed. Tombstone had been right in his estimate of their numbers. There were five of them and three already had rifles in their hands. The gunmen rode on through the trees and then splashed their horses into the stream bed, riding slowly towards them. Carson had to turn his head in order to follow them and Tombstone shifted gently. A horse neighed and then Carson became aware of another sound like a muffled castanet. It was Laura's teeth chattering. The lead rider was almost abreast of them when he raised his arm as a signal to halt. He looked about him. In the silence Carson could hear Laura breathing and then her teeth went off again. The horseman looked puzzled. He raised his rifle and peered intently into the trees. It seemed to Carson that he must see them. He glanced at Tombstone. Suddenly the horseman shouted something and in the same instant a shot rang out and a bullet screamed into the branches just over their heads. Without waiting, Carson and Tombstone leaped to their feet and began firing.

The lead horseman threw up his arms and went plunging from his saddle, his rifle flying into the air. Behind him, another rider slipped sideways into the water. Two horsemen were urging their horses back downstream and the fifth had flung himself from the saddle and rolled into cover on the other side of the stream from where he was pumping lead in the direction of Carson and Tombstone. Carson ran forward to the shelter of another tree and Tombstone slithered into some underbrush. Laura had screamed at the first report and Carson could just make out her figure lying curled up behind a tree in the shelter of undergrowth. For the moment she seemed to be safe and he shouted to her to stay exactly where she was. He had no way of knowing whether she heard him or not and for the next few moments all his attention was directed towards the battle in hand. A bullet ricocheted and went whistling uncomfortably close to his head and in the next instance a slug tore into the tree he was hiding behind, sending pieces of bark flying into his face. He felt blood running down his cheek. Tombstone's gun was booming, and stabs of flame marked where the man who had rolled from his horse was concealed. Carson fired in that direction. Jamming bullets into the chambers of his .44, he ran forward to try and get a better view of what was happening with the other gunmen. He could not see any sign of them and just then a fresh fusillade of bullets tore up the trees around him. Tombstone had rushed forward too and now he was shouting to Carson above the roar of gunfire.

'I see them! To your right!'

Carson turned his head as another burst of fire confirmed what Tombstone had said. The gunslicks had obviously ridden back down the stream where they had dismounted and were now attempting to get behind them. More shots rang out and then there was a brief lull. They seemed to have reached a temporary stalemate where no one could see anyone else. Carson decided to take a risk and draw the fire of the man sheltering on the opposite side of the stream by running into the open and exposing himself briefly to the man's gun.

'Cover me!' he yelled, and as Tombstone's gun cracked into life he dashed out from behind the tree and ran towards the stream, flinging himself forward as further stabs of flame followed by a crescendo of noise indicated to him where his assailant was concealed. Rolling to one side as he hit the earth, he returned fire and heard a sudden cry of pain from the under- growth on the other side. Meanwhile, Tombstone had opened fire behind him. Looking back, Carson had a brief sight of one of the gunmen creeping up on Tombstone. Taking aim briefly, he fired. The man flinched and then fell forward on his face, his hands clutching at the air. Below him, Carson could see the bodies of the two gunmen they had shot from their horses lying in the stream. There was a single shot from somewhere behind them and then quiet descended, made all the more palpable by contrast with the din which had preceded it. All unnoticed, the dawn had spread its first rays along the eastern horizon. Carson lay still, waiting to see what might transpire next, but there was no resumption of gunplay. The voice of Tombstone broke the silence.

'Carson, are you OK?'

'I'm OK,' he shouted back.

He thought of Laura and called to her.

'I'm all right. What's happening?' she replied.

'I ain't sure yet. Just stay where you are.'

Gingerly, Carson got to his feet, still taking care to shelter behind a tree. He heard movement and then Tombstone was at his side.

'What do you think?' he said.

'I think we've taken care of 'em,' Carson replied.

'Reckon you're right. I'm pretty sure we accounted for four of the varmints. Ain't so sure about the other.'

As if in reply to his comments, the dwindling night was suddenly disturbed by the sound of muffled hoofbeats fading into the distance.

'Yup,' Tombstone said. 'And there he goes. Reckon he's had enough.'

'You go back and take care of Miss Laura,' Carson said. 'I'll see if I can find what's happened to the others.'

'Be careful,' Tombstone warned.

Quickly Carson splashed through the stream, halting on the other side in the shelter of the undergrowth, waiting to see if there might be any further response from the gunman. Dodging his way forward, he soon saw the man sprawled behind a bush. He was badly injured. Blood was pouring from a hole in his chest and issuing from his mouth in a dark flood. Through glazed eyes he looked up at Carson, and it was clear that he was dying. Carson knelt down and cradled his head. Even in death there was an ugly leer across the man's face and in a choked voice he murmured:

'You low-down skunk.'

'Shut up,' Carson said.

He untied his neckerchief and applied it to the man's chest in a feeble effort to staunch the bleeding.

'Damn you to hell!' the man breathed. Still cursing, he coughed one more time and then his head fell back. There was nothing Carson could have done. Laying the man's head on the ground, he made his way back to the stream and checked that the two men lying in it were dead. Their horses were nowhere to be seen. They must have moved off down the streambed and into the trees. As he came up, Tombstone confirmed that the fourth gunman was dead also. Laura was holding on to him and sobbing.

'It's awful,' she said. 'Please take me home.'

Carson looked at Tombstone. He was bleeding from a scalp wound over his left ear.

'Mighty close thing,' he said. 'Creased my head but it's still in one piece. Looks like you've taken one yourself.'

'It's nothing,' Carson said, suddenly aware of the cuts to his face from the shards of bark which had flown up from the tree he had been sheltering behind. He was tempted to make a short camp. They were all exhausted and could do with some patching up, but he realized that once the gunman who had escaped met up with his fellows they would be targeted once more.

'Time to sort ourselves out later,' he said. 'Let's get to the horses and ride.'

Laura looked at him. 'What about those?' she said, pointing blindly towards the stream where the bodies lay.

'Nothing we can do,' Tombstone rejoined.

'It's horrible,' she repeated, but allowed herself to be led away from the scene.

Despite his tiredness and the exertions he had been through, Carson was still trying to figure out their next move. Daylight had surged up. The first necessity was to put distance between themselves and Carlyon's gunslicks.

7

It was turning out a fine day for Griffin and his long-time foreman Mart Adams as they rode back to the ranch after having settled some business in town. The transaction had gone well and it looked as though Griffin was about to acquire more property in Crow Bend. His influence was spreading. He had spent a very pleasant few hours at the Bird Cage. He had spoken with Cobb about the Laura Routledge affair. The marshal had seemed oddly distracted but, all in all, things were moving along very satisfactorily. Just a little more pressure on the Bar X and the other small ranches should be enough to make them fall into his hands. Then he could develop the range to the Big Ooze and beyond.

'Boss,' Adams said. 'D'you reckon Routledge and that boy of his are gonna be satisfied with things as they are? They were mighty riled yesterday. They could still cause trouble.'

'I said I'd do everything I could to help find Laura Routledge. I've spoken with the marshal. I guess that should be enough to keep them quiet.'

'You know their herd is about ready to move?'

'It's under control,' Griffin said. 'There's no way they're goin' to cash in.' Adams gave him a sharp look.

'There's bin some friction between our boys and Roach's men. I don't like it.'

'It won't be for much longer,' Griffin said.

'Did you really need to bring Roach and his boys in on all this?'

'Let's just say I kinda owed his mother a favour. You worry too much. I can deal with Roach.'

They rode on in silence. Soon the Slash H ranch house hove into view. There was smoke coming from the chimney but the yard and its surroundings seemed oddly quiet and deserted. Two of Roach's men were leaning against the bunkhouse door.

'Ain't you got nothin' to do?' Adams called.

One of them sniggered and the other one called something back. Neither of them moved.

'Take our horses,' Griffin said. 'See they're looked after.'

Neither moved immediately but after a pause one of them shrugged and came forward to take the horses' reins. Adams watched them make their way to the stable and then stepped up on to the veranda behind his boss. Griffin flung the door open and they walked inside. Seated behind the table, with his feet on the polished wood, lounged Roach. Around him half a dozen of his closest comrades were gathered. They didn't move or show any interest in Griffin's arrival.

'What is this?' Griffin said.

Roach looked around at his sidekicks. They grinned back at him.

'Get your feet off my table.'

Roach tilted his chair back a little further. He was wearing spurs and they grated against the fine table top.

'You heard what Mr Griffin said,' Adams snarled. 'Get your feet off the table.'

Roach's glance moved to the foreman.

'I heard,' he said. 'Trouble is, Griffin don't give the orders round here no more.'

Griffin looked angry. He moved forward as if to dislodge Roach physically. A gun appeared in Roach's hand.

'Now don't go and do anything hasty,' he said.

Griffin stopped and looked about him. He felt confused. 'What are you all doing here?' he said. 'This is my house. You're on my property. What the hell do you think the game is?'

'Ain't no game,' Roach said. 'Fact of the matter is the ranch is mine now. You just been relieved of the responsibility.'

'We'll see about that,' Griffin said. 'I don't know what's got into you, but I warn you. You'd better stop this right now and get out.'

'Can't be done,' Roach said.

He put the chair down to the floor and with his left hand felt in the pockets of his shirt. Pulling out a folded parchment, he flung it on the table.

'Take a look if you like. It's all legal and ratified by the marshal.'

'Are those the deeds of my property?' Griffin said. 'What are you doing with them? If I find you've been rifling through my private documents — '

'Correction. I think you mean your former property. If you care to take a look you'll see that the property has been ceded to me. As of right now the Slash H and everything to do with it belongs to me.'

Griffin was baffled and frustrated. He was at a loss to know what was going on.

'You must be mad!' he finally expostulated.

He turned to Adams. 'Come on,' he said. 'I don't intend to stay here and listen to this nonsense any further.'

He turned to go but before he had taken a step Roach's gun spat lead and he staggered forwards. Roach fired again and Griffin went down on his knees, turning a bemused eye on his foreman. Adams took a step towards him, reaching for his gun. Before it was out of its holster he was hit by a hail of bullets from Roach's men which lifted him backwards. He was dead before he crashed to the floor. Griffin managed to turn his head towards Roach but it only meant that the next bullet hit him square in the temple and he keeled over, still disbelieving, in a welter of blood. Roach blew the smoke from his weapon and placed it back in its holster. He rose from the chair and stood over the bodies of his two victims.

'Well,' he joked. 'You boys all seen what happened. It was either him or me. He left me no alternative.'

There was a burst of laughter.

'Sure, we seen it all. There was nothin' any of us could do.'

'Take 'em away,' Roach said. 'Get rid of 'em.'

Still laughing, the men stepped forward to take hold of the bodies. As they began to drag them out, Roach stopped them. He pulled a knife out of his belt.

'I almost forgot,' he said. 'Before you do that there's a little ceremony I think I ought to perform in honour of the dead.'

He bent down and seized a handful of Griffin's hair.

'Yes!' some of the men cried.

'You do it boss!'

There was general amusement as Roach added two more scalps to his collection. He held the gruesome trophies aloft as the bodies of Griffin and his foreman were dragged from the room.

'I'm leavin' you boys for now,' Roach said. 'Make yourselves comfortable.'

There was shouting and pandemonium as the gunslicks made for

Griffin's drinks cabin.

Roach laughed again. 'Leave some for me!' he shouted.

He left the ranch house and made for the stables. His horse had already been saddled and he quickly swung aboard. The two hardcases from the bunkhouse were outside.

'See you in town!' one of them called.

He turned to his companion.

'Guess we know where's he's headed.'

They both chortled and then moved over to join their companions having a party in the ranch house.

★ ★ ★

When Roach hit town he made straight for the Bird Cage. When he came through the door Canyon Kate rushed up to him.

'I wasn't expecting you,' she said.

She kissed him on the cheek but he pushed her aside.

'Where's Cindy?' he said.

'Don't be in such a hurry, son. Come

and have a drink first. I'll send Brannigan to tell Cindy to get ready.'

'It's OK, Ma,' he said. 'I'll go straight up myself and have a drink later. Tell you what. You can get the cook to make me one of his specialities.'

'What a boy!' she said. 'Always in such a rush. All right, you go on up. When you've finished I'll make you something myself.'

He went past her and up the richly carpeted stairs to the corridor above and without knocking burst into Cindy's room. She was standing by the dresser and looked up startled at his approach.

'Wesley!' she said.

Without speaking, he seized her by the shoulders and forced her down on the bed.

'Wesley,' she repeated. 'I'm not ready. Please, give me a chance — '

He slapped her hard across the face and his hand sought her skirt. She was struggling but he hit her again and she started to sob. Blood was flowing from her mouth. He had her skirt hitched up now and was pulling at her undergarments. Tugging at his belt, he wriggled out of his trousers.

'Please!' she breathed.

Her hand caught at his but there was nothing she could do to stop him.

When he had finished, he took his gun from its holster and held it to her head.

'Please!' she whimpered. 'What are you doing?'

He cocked the weapon and she shrank back against the pillow, trying to hide her face with her hands as if that would protect her. She was shaking and moaning in low anguished tones. Pushing the gun against her temple he pulled the trigger. The hammer fell on an empty chamber as she uttered a terrified scream. Laughing viciously, he put the gun back into its holster and moved to the door.

'See you later, bitch,' he hissed, slamming the door behind him. His mother was standing at the top of the stairs.

'I thought I heard a cry,' she said. 'Is everything OK?'

He walked up to her and put his arm around her shoulders.

'Everything's fine, Ma,' he said. 'Everything is just fine.'

She wouldn't be seeing that bastard Griffin any more. She didn't need him or his financial backing. From now on, he was the king. When she knew, she would be real proud of him. From now on there was just him and her. And Cindy and the other girls, of course. He smiled. He hadn't thought of it, but after all he was now the boss of the Bird Cage too.

★ ★ ★

Carson, Tombstone and Laura had crossed the Big Ooze. It didn't present much of a barrier but it seemed to them to represent a dividing line. Carson figured that Carlyon and his gang would be unlikely to pursue them further. They had their responsibilities back at the ranch and would leave it to Griffin and his henchmen to deal with them. Carson's entire concern now was to return Laura to her father. He and Tombstone would need to be careful where the marshal was concerned. Whatever their next step might be, they would need to be discreet and avoid detection. Then he remembered what Tombstone had told him about the previous marshal. They had camped towards midday, taking enough time to build a fire and make coffee. They chewed on strips of jerky.

'Tell me,' Carson said. 'What was the name of that ole marshal? The one that was in charge before Cobb took over.'

'You mean Marshal Gillespie?' Tombstone replied.

Laura looked up.

'It's funny,' she said. 'After you two rode out, when Mr Carson had recovered from his injury, I started wondering whether things might have been different if he'd still been marshal.

I don't think he would have handled things like Cobb.'

'You're right there, Miss Laura. If Gillespie was still around I reckon a lot of things might have been different.'

'Didn't you tell me he'd had a riding accident?' Carson said.

'That's what everyone believes, including Gillespie himself,' Tombstone replied. 'Some folks has their doubts.'

'How do you mean?' Laura said.

'Gillespie was no greenhorn. He'd spent most of his life in the saddle.'

'These things can happen. My horse bolted the time Mr Carson came to my assistance.'

'Whatever caused the accident,' Carson said, 'what is Gillespie doin' now?'

'When he handed in his badge he went to live with his sister. She's got a little place on the edge of town. Why do you ask?'

'I liked Mr Gillespie,' Laura commented. 'He's a good man and Crow Bend was a peaceful town while he represented the Law.'

Carson glanced at her across the fire and then addressed his next comment to Tombstone.

'Just as a matter of interest,' he said, 'was the Bird Cage in existence then?'

'The Bird Cage has been around a long time,' Tombstone replied, 'but it used to be just another saloon in those days.'

'And Canyon Kate?'

'She's been around a long time too. Started off there as a barmaid. Used to put on a bit of a show sometimes; you know, a few songs, a bit of dancin'. Eventually she became the proprietor but not like she is now.'

'Interestin',' Carson said. 'But to go back to what we were saying, it seems to me that there ain't goin' to be no law and order while Cobb is the marshal, especially if he's in the pay of Griffin.'

Tombstone thought for a moment. 'Well, if Cobb ain't the man for the job then the sensible thing would be to bring back the man who is.'

'And that man's Gillespie,' Carson said.

'Goldurn it, you're right. That upstart Cobb should never have been marshal in the first place.'

'How do you reckon the townsfolk would feel about havin' Gillespie back?' Carson said.

Tombstone laughed. 'That don't take no thinkin' about. Folks were plumb upset and disappointed when he handed in his badge. They'd form a reception committee if there was any chance of gettin' him back.' He paused.

'By Jiminy!' he continued, 'it's worth a try. Most folks still think of him as the real law around town. If we can put Gillespie right about what's been happenin', what with Griffin hirin' a bunch of gunslicks an' the rustlin' an' all, not to mention what happened to Miss Laura, I think we might just be able to put that no-good sidewinder Cobb in his place.'

'Are you certain that Griffin was involved in what happened to me?'

Laura said. She still could not quite believe that Griffin would stoop so low.

'Him or some of his men,' Carson replied. 'Makes no difference in the end. As for Gillespie, it's up to us to try and convince him that he's needed. But first we got to get you back to the ranch.'

★ ★ ★

It was late in the afternoon when they reached the Bar X. Routledge must have seen them coming because he ran into the yard and flung himself upon Laura as she climbed wearily from the saddle. Lou Reynolds came out of the bunkhouse to lend his assistance. Rik was out on the range but Routledge gave orders to tell him the news and Clem Shorter went galloping off.

'What happened? Are you all right? Are you hurt?' Routledge was asking a host of questions but his overriding sense of relief was obvious. Laura tried to calm him down.

'Don't fuss,' she said. 'I'm fine, thanks to Mr Carson and Tombstone.' Routledge turned and wrung both their hands.

'Thank you, thank you,' he breathed. 'How can I ever repay you for finding my daughter?'

Laura smiled. 'Mr Carson in particular seems to be making a habit of it,' she said.

Over coffee, Laura told her father what had happened to her out on the range. As she spoke his anger grew and it was with difficulty that they managed to restrain him.

'If Griffin is behind all this,' he said, 'I'll kill him.'

Just then Rik burst through the door and Laura had to briefly repeat what she had told her father. He turned to Carson and Tombstone, his face etched with emotion.

'We owe you, Carson,' he said. 'And Tombstone, you've got a place here for life.'

When Rik had regained control of himself and sat next to his sister, Carson began to explain what he and Tombstone had found.

'I knew it,' Rik breathed. 'I knew Griffin would be behind all the rustlin' and all the stock we been losin'.'

Routledge had jumped to his feet. 'Who would have believed it?' he said. 'A whole operation goin' on beyond the Big Ooze.'

'I reckon we got all the proof we need,' Rik said. 'Why don't I round up the boys and we'll take a ride.'

'Hold it just a minute,' Carson said. 'I'm right with you and we all agree it's about time Griffin was stopped. But before you go off at half-cock there's a little something Tombstone and I want to sort out.'

He told them about his plans to try and get the former marshal's backing.

'I've known Gillespie a long time,' Routledge said. 'He'd be a good man to have along.'

He turned to Carson. 'Like my son

says, we owe you, Carson. We'll go along with your plan. But let me ride with you to see the old buzzard.'

'Sounds fine by me. Now, have you had any further visits from Marshal Cobb? Remember, as far as he's concerned, Tombstone and me are still wanted men.'

'Nope,' Routledge replied. 'There's a few posters bin put up in town but that's about it.'

'Then if it's OK by you, I suggest we all get some rest tonight and get down to it in the mornin'. The three of us are just about bushed.'

Laura allowed her father and brother to lead her to the bedroom where Carson had been during his convalescence. Carson and Tombstone would have been happy with their bunks but Routledge insisted on them staying for the night at the ranch house. After they had eaten, they enjoyed some of Routledge's best whiskey and cigars. Then they spent the night between sheets.

'Sure is nice,' Tombstone said. 'But I still got a sort of hankerin' after the old line cabin. Wish I had a book to read.'

'What about that there Trojan horse critter you started tellin' me about,' Carson replied.

Tombstone lay on his back looking up at the ceiling. 'Well now,' he began. 'That old hoss was a skewbald just like Cleo.'

There was a snore from Carson's corner of the room.

'Guess I ain't just tellin' it right,' Tombstone said to himself.

★   ★   ★

Jim Gillespie lived with his sister Ada. She had a pleasant little house near the edge of town with a small piece of garden and a whitewashed fence. Sister and brother were sitting together on the veranda when Carson and Routledge came down the dusty lane to their front gate. They had left Tombstone in charge of the horses

176

outside of town. Ada Gillespie was the first to notice them.

'Why, if it ain't Mister Routledge,' she said.

Her brother got to his feet as Routledge and Carson came up to the veranda.

'Gillespie,' Routledge said, offering his hand. 'It's good to see you. I'd like to introduce you to a friend of mine, Mr Jack Carson.'

Carson and the ex-marshal shook hands. Carson tipped his hat to Ada.

'Let's go inside,' she said. 'I'm sure you could both handle a drink?'

Inside, the house was neat and clean with hand-stitched cushions and bowls of flowers around the room. Ada went into the kitchen, presently returning with three glasses of whiskey and water on a tray. Carson was touched by the air of respectful familiarity with which she treated the rancher. It was obvious that they were all old friends and liked each other's company.

'Here's to you,' Routledge said,

raising his glass and addressing the ex-marshal.

They each took a drink.

'All right, Routledge,' Gillespie said. 'I know you've got something up your sleeve. Come on, out with it. What really brings you here?'

'Jim, I'm sure it's just a friendly visit. Isn't that so, Mr Routledge?' Ada said, but there was a gleam in her eye too.

Routledge swallowed another drink and then laughed. 'I can't hide anything from you two, can I?' he said. 'Of course, you're quite right. We do have an ulterior motive in visiting, but it's not entirely selfish.'

He turned to Carson. 'This is your show,' he said. 'Perhaps you'd better do the explaining.'

Carson put his glass down on a table top, but before he could say anything the marshal spoke.

'Gentlemen,' he said, 'the answer's yes.'

They all looked at each other.

'I don't get you,' Routledge said.

'Nobody's said anything yet.'

A smile had spread across Gillespie's sharp features. 'Then let me say it,' he said. 'I might be an old duffer and way out of my time, but I ain't exactly lost my marbles yet.'

'And that's a matter of opinion,' his sister broke in.

'I bin takin' it easy of late and I guess I kinda' enjoy it in a way. But lately I bin figurin' maybe I let myself be put out to grazin' a mite early. It's nice here. Nobody bothers us. But I can see what's bin goin' on and I sure as hell know that young upstart Cobb ain't fit to wear the star. After all those years upholdin' the law, a man takes a sort of pride in what he's done. This is a nice town. It's a good country. I'd like to think it was at least partly down to my doin' that it's shaped up that way. Now I can see it's startin' to go down the pan and, to be truthful, I ain't too happy about it.'

'Just lately he's been like a flea on a leash,' Ada put in.

'So you know what's been worryin' us?' Routledge said.

'Same thing's bin worryin' me. I seen some low-down trash hangin' about town. I've heard rumours. I seen Rik lookin' worried and I know you got a herd of longhorns just about ready to start up the trail.'

'There's something more definite than rumours now,' Routledge said. 'Go on, Carson, tell him what you found.'

Carson took a long swallow of his drink. 'It's like this,' he began.

When he had finished the ex-marshal leaped to his feet.

'Well,' he said, 'that about confirms all my suspicions. I had a feelin' that Griffin was no good. It's about time somebody stood up to him.'

'So you're with us,' Routledge snapped.

'All the way. Man, I sure am glad you come out here today and told me all this.'

Gillespie seemed like a man rejuvenated as he paced up and down the carpet. He turned to Ada. 'You see, don't you?' he said. 'I can't just sit back any longer and ignore things.'

Ada shook her head as if her brother was one more incorrigible schoolboy like the ones she once used to teach.

'I've just been waiting for this moment,' she replied. 'I could see you were getting restless but I didn't know what to do to get you to realize your own feelings.'

She turned from her brother to Routledge and Carson. 'I don't know about him,' she said, 'but I'm for sure glad you took the time to visit. I don't know what you've got in mind but just take him off my hands.'

Gillespie strode over and lifted his sister bodily out of the chair. 'What would I do without you?' he said. 'You know me better than I know myself.'

'Put me down this instant!' she exclaimed.

When the ex-marshal had restored her to her feet, she looked again at Routledge and Carson. 'Just make sure you bring him back in one piece,' she said.

'Sure will,' Routledge replied.

'You say that Tombstone is out there holdin' on to the hosses,' Gillespie said. 'I guess the old coyote will be wonderin' what's become of us. Why don't we get back to the Bar X and decide what we aim to do?'

'Just what I was about to suggest,' Routledge replied.

Gillespie strode across the room to where a gun rack hung on the wall. He took down a rifle and then buckled on his gunbelt.

'Never felt rightly dressed recently till now,' he said.

Carson and Routledge took their farewells of Ada. The marshal was saddling up his horse. They circled around the outskirts of town and, after a short walk through some brush, saw the figure of Tombstone with the Appaloosa and the skewbald. When Gillespie joined them they hoisted themselves into the saddle and headed away from town. They hadn't gone far when Carson's keen eyes spotted something in the distance.

'Looks like a body,' Tombstone said.

'Let's take a closer look,' Gillespie added.

Taking a short detour, they approached the figure which lay sprawled face down on the grass. They could see now that it was a woman.

'Laura!' Routledge gasped, fearing the worst as he leaped from the saddle. Rushing across, he turned the girl over. 'Thank God,' he said. 'It isn't Laura.'

Carson was right behind him. 'I know her. She's one of the girls from the Bird Cage. I think her name is Cindy.'

The girl had been badly beaten. Her face was cut and bruised and there was a gap in her mouth where two of her teeth had been broken, but she was still alive.

'Be careful, she may have other injuries,' Carson said. 'Help me get her up on my horse.'

'We'll take her back to the ranch,' Routledge said.

'Whoever did this to her,' Carson muttered, 'is going to pay.'

All of them felt the same surge of anger and disgust. As gently as possible they lifted her on to Carson's horse. As they did so her eyes flickered open and she moaned.

'I wonder what she's doin' out here?' Tombstone mused.

There was no indication of a horse, no tracks or any other sign.

'Looks to me like she must have been on foot. Maybe she was tryin' to get away from someone,' Gillespie said.

'Reckon you're right,' Carson hissed. 'And I think I've got a pretty good idea who.'

'You thinkin' of your man Roach?' Tombstone said.

Carson nodded. His jaw was set and his mouth was a thin line. 'Just one more thing he's gonna have to answer for,' he snarled.

Gillespie was looking closely at

Carson. The name of Roach had come up during the explanations back at his sister's house. He was reflecting that if Carson was right, he wouldn't like to be in Roach's shoes once Carson finally caught up with him.

8

For a few days, things were relatively quiet. The doctor came out from town to visit the girl they had found beaten up. Her injuries were worse than they had even suspected. She had cracked ribs and severe bruises to her body where someone had kicked her and was lucky not to have a punctured lung. She would recover but it would take time.

'Those injuries are deliberately inflicted,' the doctor said. 'What kind of person would do this?'

She was frightened and reluctant to talk. Eventually it was Laura who won her confidence sufficiently for her to tell something of what had happened and it confirmed what Carson had suspected. From what little she said it seemed that Roach had inflicted the injuries on her after a bad-tempered drunken session at the Bird Cage. He had left her unconscious and when she came round it was the early hours of the morning. Summoning what strength she could muster she had succeeded in escaping from the Bird Cage and making her way out of town. Roach's abuse had grown steadily worse. She had tried in earlier days to appeal to Canyon Kate but she had not realized then that Canyon Kate was his mother.

'Poor girl,' Laura said to her father. 'It seems she's had an awful time. We can't let her go back to the Bird Cage.'

'It might be best if she moved away from Crow Bend altogether,' her father replied. 'I have some contacts. Leave it to me.'

While the doctor was at the ranch he checked up on Laura herself. She was still quite shaken by what she had gone through and he prescribed her a sedative. Afterwards, he asked, 'How is Mr Carson? I take it he's fully recovered from his wounds.'

He went out the door and climbed into his buggy. As he drove away he observed ex-marshal Gillespie coming out of the bunkhouse. *Well there's a thing*, he thought to himself. *I wonder what old Jim Gillespie is doing at the Bar X? Looks like I might be needed yet awhiles.*

★   ★   ★

The cattle drive had started. Rik didn't want to delay things any longer. His sister was safe and he felt reasonably happy about things at the ranch. As yet, no hint of events at the Slash H had reached their ears. So far as anyone was aware, Griffin was still in charge. The Slash H boss had been pushing them hard but Rik was still to be convinced there would be any threat from Griffin on the trail. Just in case they might be needed, however, the men wore six-guns and carried rifles.

The day after the start of the trail drive Gillespie and Routledge rode into town, the former to call on his sister, the latter to see Marshal Cobb.

Although nobody expected the marshal to do anything, they had decided to follow the letter of the law and present to him the facts concerning Roach's assault on the girl Cindy from the Bird Cage. Tying his horse to the hitch rail outside the marshal's office, Routledge mounted the steps to the boardwalk and knocked on the marshal's door. Pinned to it was a Wanted poster for Carson and Tombstone. He didn't pause for an answer but turned the handle and strode in. Marshal Cobb was sitting at his desk reading through some papers. He looked up at the ranch owner's approach.

'Well if it ain't Mr Routledge,' he said. 'This is a pleasure.'

'I'm here strictly on business,' Routledge replied.

'As you can see, the office is open. Take a seat. What can I do for you?'

Routledge lowered himself on to a wooden chair on the opposite side of the desk. The marshal shuffled the papers he had been looking at before placing them in a drawer.

'Do you know a young lady by the name of Cindy who works at the Bird Cage?'

'Now what sort of a question is that?' Marshal Cobb began but, seeing the intense look on Routledge's face, he changed his tone.

'Sure, I know her. Her proper name is Cinnamon. She's one of Kate's girls. Has there been some sort of complaint about her?'

'There's been no complaint,' Routledge said. 'If anything, just the opposite. Fact of the matter is I was riding with some of my men when we found her very badly beaten out on the range. She'll survive, but it was a near thing. She's frightened and didn't want to talk but in the end she named her attacker.'

'Yeah? And who might that be?'

'A low-down snake by the name of Wesley Roach.'

'Is she quite sure about that?'

'Why would she lie? Her injuries are

real enough. Ask the doctor.'

'Do I understand that you're privy to this girl's whereabouts?'

'If you mean by that do I know where she is, there ain't no question about that. Right now she's out at my ranch doing her best to make a recovery.'

The marshal puffed out his cheeks. 'So, let me get this right. You state yourself that you have a young lady of dubious reputation staying at your ranch. She happens to be carryin' some injuries and you say she's blamin' 'em on the son of the proprietor of one of the best-known establishments in town.'

'That's not what I said,' Routledge replied.

'OK, maybe not in so many words. But tell me, where exactly do I fit into this?'

Routledge was trying to keep his temper.

'You're the representative of law and order. I expect you to arrest this Roach and put him behind bars.'

The marshal's eyes opened wide and

he gave out a hollow laugh.

'Now just hold it right there,' he said. 'In the first place, I've only got your say so for any of this. In the second place, even if the young woman's injuries aren't self-inflicted, there's no sayin' who might have done it. It's her word against anyone else's. Who's to say one of your boys isn't responsible? And in the third place, it ain't some good-for-nothin' cowboy she's accusin'. Nope sirree! It just happens to be one of the most prominent members of Crow Bend society.'

'What the hell do you mean? I gather that this Roach is the son of Canyon Kate but that sure don't mean anything. From what I can gather, he and some of his friends have been causing a heap of trouble since he arrived back in town.'

Marshal Cobb leaned back in his chair. 'If I were you I'd be a bit careful what you say. In point of fact, this man, Wesley Roach that you seem to have such a poor opinion of, is now the rightful owner of the biggest spread in the territory, the Slash H, not to mention a sizeable chunk of property right here in town.'

Routledge was staggered. 'How can that be? Otis Griffin is the owner of the Slash H. Just what are you trying to tell me?'

'You should get into town more often,' the marshal said. 'Out there at the Bar X you just ain't in touch with events. Unfortunately, Mr Griffin recently passed away. In consideration of all the help Mr Roach has been to him in his last days, he has deeded the ranch to him, doubtless in the belief that he is the right man to carry forward his legacy.'

'Is this some kind of joke?' Routledge replied.

'It's no joke. In fact, to quote your own words, it's just the opposite. Those papers I put in the drawer are a copy of all the relevant paperwork being held at the offices of Mr Randall Murray, attorney at law and respected elder citizen of this town.'

'A two-bit, cheatin' pen pusher,' Routledge responded.

Marshal Cobb rose to his feet. 'There you go again, slanderin' folk. I'm afraid I am not prepared to hear good people, friends and neighbours, abused in that fashion. You may not like what you have heard, but it's all signed, sealed and legal. As for this other matter you broached, the lady is a whore. If you choose to associate yourself with her lies, that's your prerogative. I hate to be inhospitable but I'm afraid I must ask you to leave.'

Routledge got to his feet.

'If that's your last word, Marshal, I shall be on my way. But don't think people aren't getting wise to you and to what's been going on around here recently. Don't imagine that you're going to get away with it for much longer.'

'I will ignore your threats,' Cobb replied. 'And by the way,' he added as Routledge opened the door, 'I expect you noticed that Wanted poster. I wouldn't like to think you might be tempted to harbour known fugitives. Don't force me into an invidious position where I should find it necessary to act against you.'

Routledge slammed the door. Behind him, the marshal broke into a peal of laughter. Routledge forced himself not to react. After all, the marshal's attitude was what he had expected. But he hadn't expected the news about Wesley Roach. He could still hardly believe it. He wondered what Jack Carson would think about it.

* * *

Wesley Roach was at that very moment back at the Slash H, having spent the previous night at the Bird Cage. As he sat on the porch admiring his new-found domain, one of his gunslicks rode into the yard. He seemed excited and the condition of his horse indicated that he had ridden it hard.

'Boss,' he said, 'I got news.'

'Is that so?' Roach replied, spitting out a gob of tobacco juice. 'Now why don't you just calm down and then say what you got to say.'

'It's about the Bar X. They've moved the herd out.'

A faint smile spread across the mean features of the new owner of the Slash H.

'Good,' he said. 'It's what I bin waitin' for.'

'What you got in mind, boss?'

Roach's grin grew wider. 'What do you think?' he said. He jumped to his feet. 'We got the Slash H. How would you feel about addin' the Bar X?' The man wasn't very bright and he looked blankly back at Roach.

'Hell, I sometimes wonder . . . ' Roach began. He stopped and seemed to reach a decision.

'I ain't hangin' about,' he said. 'Round up the boys and tell 'em to be ready day after tomorrow. We're gonna hit that herd and hit it hard. Those cow critters are gonna make us some money. We'll clean out Routledge and his bunch of no-good cowpokes once an' for all.'

The man looked hesitant.

'Git yourself a new hoss,' Roach snapped. 'And get goin'. By the way, who's in charge of the drive?'

'Seems like it's Rik Routledge,' the man replied.

Roach's grin became a positive leer. Rik Routledge, the boss's son. He would make a good scalp for the collection. Now he had taken the decision to attack the herd he was almost inclined to take off at once, but he would let them get a little way along the trail, just enough so the riders would be getting tired while the cattle were bedding in. He'd leave a few of the boys behind and besides, he had Marshal Cobb to handle any eventualities. Carson was still a wanted man. It would be the icing on the cake to see him behind bars again, him and that other hombre whose cabin they had burned down. No, hanging them afterwards would be the icing on the cake. He laughed out loud as he strode into the ranch house.

★ ★ ★

While Routledge and the ex-marshal were in town, Carson was making himself useful digging post holes for a new pen. Standing erect, he pushed his hat back off his forehead and let his gaze sweep across the open range. It was good country. Beyond the Big Ooze there was plenty of room for expansion. Carson found himself thinking of what might be achieved with a lot of dedication and hard work.

Preoccupied with his thoughts, he scarcely noticed a rider approaching. As the figure drew nearer he saw it was Laura. She was wearing a cream blouse with her brown riding habit and a brown hat which only partly concealed her cascades of dark auburn hair. Carson observed for the first time a few freckles over her nose and the line of her parted lips. His heart was beating.

'Miss Laura,' he said. 'Should you be riding on your own?'

He stepped forward to assist her from the saddle.

'It's not far,' she replied. 'Besides, I can't let what happened stop me. And just in case, I now carry this with me wherever I go.'

She reached into the recesses of her jacket and produced a double-barrelled .41 calibre rimfire pistol.

'That ain't likely to be a lot of use less'n you're real close and not up against a movin' target.'

She shrugged. 'I know how to use it,' she said.

Carson felt a little uncomfortable and decided to switch the conversation from the direction it was taking.

'Is your father back from town?' he asked.

'Not yet,' she replied. 'I thought he might have returned by now.'

'Guess he's plenty of things to see to.'

'He went in with Mr Gillespie. They've probably taken time to visit his sister. She's a sweet old lady. Do you know she used to teach me? I was only a kid in those days and she was near to retirement even then.'

She turned to the old speckled roan she was riding and, feeling in its saddle-bags, produced a bottle and a small parcel.

'I'm afraid it's only apple juice and eggs and ham but there's a nice slice of apple pie in there as well,' she said.

'You shouldn't have taken the trouble,' Carson replied, 'but I sure could do it justice.'

The Appaloosa was tethered nearby and he went over to get a blanket which he spread on the ground.

'It ain't the most fittin' thing for a lady but it's all I can offer.'

'It's just fine,' she replied and sat down gently. 'Won't you join me?'

He lay down next to her, propping himself up on one arm. She had taken her hat off and as she shook her head her long hair spread out and hung in heavy folds to her shoulders. She had brought two cups and she poured the apple juice, proffering him one.

'To the Bar X,' she said.

She raised her glass and he did the same in return. She was smiling and there were two dimples on either side of her mouth. Her eyes sparkled. Carson became conscious of how he must look to her, hot and sweating and generally dishevelled from his labours. The sun was warm but a freshening breeze ran across the grass.

'I was just thinkin' before you arrived what a fine country this is,' he said.

'It's a lovely country,' she replied. 'I would hate to ever have to leave it.'

'Well, I guess you don't have to worry about that,' Carson replied. 'You have a good spread, the land will pass on down to you and your brother.'

'Maybe,' she said. 'But things haven't been the same since Mr Griffin arrived.' She paused before resuming on a different tack. 'And what about you, Mr

Carson? How long do you intend staying around these parts?'

Her words caught him by surprise and for some reason he struggled for an answer. She was looking into his eyes and he felt strangely unsettled. He had a tingling sensation in his chest.

'I don't know,' he said lamely. 'I guess I've always lived kinda one day at a time.'

'That's not a bad philosophy,' she said. 'Maybe we all worry too much about the future. After all, a beautiful day like today is unique; it only comes but once and then it's gone forever.'

'I never looked it that way, but of course you're right.'

She was close to him and he was very conscious of her warm, physical presence. Her perfume wafted softly on the breeze. A strand of hair blew against his shoulder.

'Yes, you're absolutely right,' he continued, when she put a finger to his lips.

'Why don't you just stop talking and

kiss me?' she said.

For a moment longer he hesitated and then something seemed to break inside him and his mouth was pressed to hers while he held her closely in his arms. For what seemed a long time they remained that way till their lips finally parted.

'Laura,' he began but got no further as she took his face and lowered it down to her own. They kissed again and he held her firmly in his arms, knowing that he had desired her from the start and that whatever the future might hold it had to include her.

'Laura, I love you,' he gasped, and she smiled as she looked into his eyes and replied simply:

'I love you too.'

For a long time they lay entwined in each other's arms before eventually moving apart.

'I must be going back,' she said, 'or they'll start worrying and wondering where I am.'

She began to smooth out the creases

in her skirt while Carson got to his feet.

'I'll ride back with you,' he said.

'I'm afraid I interfered with your digging,' she said.

'It'll wait.'

They kissed again before getting on their horses and setting off for the ranch. They both felt relaxed and happy but as they got closer to the Bar X Carson began to feel a little uncomfortable. He moved his Appaloosa up closer to the speckled roan.

'Laura,' he said.

She turned to him with a smiling face. 'Yes, Jack? You look a little worried. What is it?'

'Well,' Carson began, 'I was just wonderin' — ' He broke off and Laura looked at him quizzically.

'Yes,' she said. 'You were wondering. Wondering about what?'

Carson shifted uneasily in the saddle. 'Well,' he continued, 'I was just wonderin' about you and me. I mean, how do we go about things once we get back to the ranch? This is all kinda new to me.'

204

Laura laughed. 'It's new to me as well,' she said.

'But what about your father? What about Rik?'

'Rik's off with the herd,' she said. 'And as for my father, leave him to me.'

'But how will he take things?' Carson said. 'Let's face it, I'm new around here. Basically I'm just one of his employees. I wouldn't blame him for thinkin' I maybe ain't got a lot to offer a girl like you.'

'A girl like me,' she mimicked and laughed again. 'You do talk some nonsense, Mr Carson. You're a lot more than just an employee. He's taken to you. Trust me; there won't be any problem. In fact, you'll be doing him a favour. I reckon I've been proving more than a handful for him just recently and I'm sure he's been wondering what to do with me.'

It was Carson's turn to laugh. 'I hope you're right,' he said.

As it turned out, Carson need not have worried himself on that score. As they dismounted in the yard Routledge came out of the ranch house. His look was agitated and it was quite evident that something was in the air. If there was anything different about his daughter and Carson, he did not appear to notice it.

'I was just going to send for you,' he said to Carson, 'but now there's no need. Come right in, both of you.'

Carson and Laura exchanged glances as they made their way into the ranchhouse. Gillespie was standing by the table and they were surprised to see Tombstone there as well.

'Let's all take a seat,' Routledge said.

'What is it, Father?' Laura asked. 'You're getting me worried. It's nothing to do with Rik, is it? He hasn't had an accident?'

'It's nothing to do with Rik,' her father replied.

When they had all settled down he proceeded to tell them what the marshal had said about the demise of Griffin and the information that Wesley

Roach had taken over the Slash H. When he had finished they looked at each other in astonishment.

'I even saw something of the documents granting ownership to Roach,' Routledge said. 'Seems the marshal has a copy of them that he keeps in a top drawer.'

'I don't suppose our friend the marshal gave any indication how all this happened?' Carson said.

'Nope, not in so many words. All he said was that Griffin had passed away and left everything to Roach.'

'Sure seems more than a coincidence that Griffin dies and Roach benefits. Hasn't Roach only been working for the Slash H a short time?'

'I'd be willin' to bet that Griffin's death was no accident,' Tombstone said. 'I reckon Griffin bit off more than he could chew.'

'Yup, it sure looks like Griffin made a big mistake when he brought in Roach and his gunslicks. Probably was holdin' 'em back for some sort of showdown if his plans didn't work out,' Routledge commented.

'Or just the threat of trouble to help them along,' Gillespie added. 'And I s'pose settin' up Cobb as marshal was all part of it. With Cobb in his back pocket he would have less to worry about.'

'Question is,' Routledge concluded, 'what do we do about it now? I think we're all agreed we can't let Roach go any further. We've tried lawful means but it hasn't worked. There's no chance of Cobb doin' anything, so I guess it's up to us now.'

'Yup,' Carson said, 'I reckon you're right. I say it's time we took a ride over to the Slash H. And whatever happens after that, make sure you leave Roach to me.'

Laura threw a concerned look towards Carson. 'Please be careful, all of you,' she said.

She looked at Carson once more and then moved towards the bedroom to check on the convalescent girl. Cindy

208

was sitting up in bed but her face was still badly bruised. Looking at the damage Roach had caused, a surge of anger welled up in Laura. She half wished she could be riding with the others now the time had come to deal with Roach and his gang at the Slash H.

9

Although it was almost noon there were few signs of activity as the men from the Bar X approached the Slash H ranch house. It seemed strange that no one had challenged them and the place seemed almost deserted.

'I don't like it,' Tombstone said. 'There should be someone around.'

They had passed groups of cattle bearing the Slash H brand but there was no sign of round-up or branding going on.

'If you ask me,' Routledge said, 'Roach just don't care. Give it time and the place will go to rack and ruin. But he'll do what he can to bring us down first.'

'Less'n we stop him,' Tombstone said.

They rode into the ranch house yard.

'Roach!' Routledge called. 'Are you there?'

They sat their horses, looking about with puzzled expressions on their faces.

'Could be a set-up,' Gillespie said.

'Roach!' Routledge called again. 'We got some business to discuss.'

There was no reply from the ranch but the door of the bunkhouse swung open and a man emerged. Routledge recognized him as one of Griffin's men.

'Roach ain't here,' he said. 'What can I do for you gentlemen?'

Routledge slid out of the saddle.

'You work for Roach now?'

The man shrugged his shoulders. 'Mr Roach owns the place since Mr Griffin died. Guess I do at that.'

'What about the rest of Griffin's cowboys?'

'Some of them stayed, some of them gone. Mr Roach has his own men.'

Routledge looked about him. 'Seems mighty quiet. Where is everybody?'

'Mr Roach and most of his boys rode out early this mornin'. I didn't ask no questions.'

'Did they say when they'd be back?'

The man shook his head. 'Ain't none of my business.'

'And they didn't say where they were headed?'

'Just rode on out. There was a big gatherin' of 'em last night, though. Got pretty rowdy. I decided I'd do best to keep outa things.'

Routledge turned to the others. 'What do you think?' he said. 'Do we stick around or maybe head for town?'

They were thoughtful for a moment and then Carson whistled.

'I think I've got it,' he snapped. 'They've gone after the cattle drive! Roach has taken up where Griffin left off. It's just the sort of caper would appeal to him and his desperadoes.'

He turned to Griffin's man. 'Are you sure you're not holdin' somethin' back?'

'I've told you everythin' I know. Mr Roach sure don't tell me what all his plans are.'

Routledge put his foot in the stirrup and swung into the saddle.

'Carson's right,' he said. 'We'd better hit leather.'

* * *

Out on the range, Rik was riding the last watch before daylight. Somewhere in the darkness he could hear Lou Reynolds's low voice as he crooned to the cattle. They were circling the herd in opposite directions and soon their paths would cross. The night was still dark. There were no stars and the only light was the faint glow of the lantern on the tongue of the chuck-wagon. All the previous afternoon the herd had been nervous and jittery. Rik had told the wrangler to hobble the horses and keep them close to camp and warned the rest of the boys to be ready to move quickly if anything broke. He didn't know why he felt edgy but he was taking his cue from the cattle. In the darkness, a cow coughed and a black shape moved out of the shadows. Swinging his horse towards it, he edged

213

it back into the herd. He rode slowly and presently the dim shape of Lou Reynolds's horse loomed up out of the blackness.

'Everything OK?' Rik said softly.

Lou's head nodded.

'Take it slow and gentle,' Rik said. 'Be careful not to do anythin' that might spook 'em. They still seem a mite restless.'

'Sure thing,' Lou replied.

They continued riding, letting their horses go at their own pace, barely needing to touch the bridle reins. Rik was looking out for the first signs of dawn and allowing himself to think of breakfast — black coffee and sourdough biscuits with meat and gravy. Not too long to go.

Suddenly he came to attention, straining his ears to listen. Away off in the distance he thought he could hear a low rumble. It passed and then seemed to come again. Rik looked towards the horizon. The sky was black. Maybe it was a faraway roll of thunder he had heard. Then it came again and he knew it wasn't thunder but the drumming of horses' hoofs. At the same moment Lou Reynolds rode up again.

'You heard it too?' he said.

'Riders,' Rik snapped. 'Plenty of 'em. And they can't be up to no good.'

The sound of galloping hoofs was unmistakable now and getting louder.

'Roust up the men,' Rik said. 'We'll have a stampede on our hands.'

As if in response to his words, the cows began to move. Getting to their feet, some started to bawl and confusion spread rapidly till there was a concerted rush and they were gone, crashing away into the darkness. As Rik wheeled his horse in pursuit, the night was punctured by stabs of flame and the roar of guns. He rode fast in an effort to gain a position alongside the lead cattle, using his slicker as a flail. Other riders were coming up alongside, turning their horses in close to the plunging mass of longhorns. The cattle were circling but it was less because of the actions of the cowboys than the herd's own instinct to run against the wind. Rik tore on, thankful that he had chosen a good night horse. The herd showed little sign of slowing its pace but had settled into a steady run. Rik felt that they were getting the beasts under control when there came a fresh burst of gunfire from behind and the terrified cattle reacted by splitting into sections. For a while they continued to run parallel to each other but then, despite the efforts of the cowhands to merge them back together, they began to scatter all over the prairie. Clem Shorter came alongside.

'What the hell is happenin?' he shouted.

Rik turned to see other riders coming up. There were high shrill whoops followed by gunshots. A bullet screamed through the air over his head. A man on a horse came sweeping past, firing as he rode. Rik lifted his pistol and fired back and the man's horse went down, hurling its rider over its head into the path of a group of galloping longhorns. Rik heard the man's scream above all the other noise and commotion. It was hard for him now to make much sense of what was happening. The herd was spreading but the group of cattle he was alongside was slowing down, beginning to circle aimlessly. It was a shambles of trampling beasts but between them, Rik and Clem finally got the cattle halted.

'Stay with them,' Rik said. 'I'll see if I can locate any others.'

Rik rode off. Soon afterwards he met with some of the hands driving small bunches of cattle. At last the sky began to lighten and after a time the chuck-wagon appeared with another Bar X man hazing in what remained of the remuda. As dawn broke they brought together what cattle they had managed to find. It wasn't many. Rik was thankful that at least nobody had been killed. Clancy Moore had taken a bullet in the shoulder and another one in the leg. Two others had been injured in falls to their horses. The mangled body of the man whose horse Rik had shot was found later on the prairie. Rik examined the dead horse. It was unbranded.

The dejected crew ate a breakfast of biscuit and cold bacon before roping fresh horses and setting out to scout the prairie, finding a few scattered cattle which they rounded up to bring back to camp. Most of the herd, though, was gone. All of the men were dog tired and sore after the night's events. Rain began to fall as the cook came up once more with the chuck-wagon. He lit a fire and this time there was hot food to go with the coffee. It made them feel a little better.

'What now, boss?' one of the men said.

Rik was angry. Without the money from the sale of the herd the position of the Bar X and the other two ranches was hopeless.

'It must be the Slash H behind this,' Rik said.

'Whoever it is, they got to get rid of

those cow critters,' Clem Shorter commented.

'If we get on their tail we should be able to pick up where they're headed.'

Suddenly there was a warning yell.

'Riders! Comin' on fast!'

The men were instantly on the move, drawing their guns ready for a fight.

'Hold on!' Rik shouted. 'That looks like my father!'

'And ain't that Tombstone and Carson ridin' with him?'

A cheer of relief went up. The men had assumed that the gang of rustlers had returned. The riders came up fast and, drawing their horses to a halt, jumped to the ground.

'Rik, are you OK?' his father gasped.

'I'm OK and so are most of the boys but the cattle are gone.'

Routledge cursed. 'Too late,' he said. 'Tell me what happened, Rik.'

They gathered about the camp fire and swapped stories.

'We got here just as fast as we could once we realized what Roach's game was,' Routledge said. 'Pity we couldn't have made it a little sooner.'

'They can't have got far,' Carson said. 'We won't have any problems catchin' up with 'em.'

'Reckon they'll be makin' for the railhead?'

'It's a ways to go. If that was their aim, they'd have waited before hittin' the herd. It's a long story, but we found a place on the other side of the Big Ooze where Griffin has been drivin' some of the rustled cows. I figure they'll head back that way.'

Tombstone had been silent, drinking coffee from a battered tin cup. Now he looked up at Carson.

'I got an idea,' he said.

'Yup,' Carson replied. 'Just so long as it doesn't involve wearing eye patches or usin' fake keys.'

Gillespie gave him a puzzled look.

'Another long story,' Carson said. 'I'll tell you later. OK, Tombstone, let's hear it.'

'If you're right,' Tombstone said, 'why

don't we just leave a couple of men here to look after the cattle we got and the rest of us ride to the Big Ooze ahead of the rustlin' varmints. We'll be there as a kind of welcomin' committee.'

Carson thought it over. 'You know, I think you got somethin',' he concluded.

'Seems a good idea,' Gillespie said. 'That way we get those coyotes to do the trail drivin' for us. Sorta reverses the situation, if you see what I mean.'

For the first time since Carson had known him, a smile spread across Rik's features.

'Yup, I sure do,' he said.

'You say there are some of Roach's outfit down there already,' Gillespie reminded them.

'I hadn't forgotten,' Carson replied, 'but it works out pretty well. At present, Roach's men are divided. We can deal with the scum who are there first before settlin' with Roach and the rest of 'em.'

They looked at one another.

'What are we waitin' for?' Rik said. 'Let's head for the Big Ooze.'

* ★ ★ ★

Whichever way the stolen herd was being driven, nothing was seen of it as they reached the Big Ooze and crossed to the other side. It didn't bother them. There would be time and enough to retake the herd. Occasionally they came upon stray longhorns which proved to carry the Bar X brand when Rik Routledge checked them out.

'Thievin' varmints,' his father snapped. 'They deserve everything that's coming to them.'

They continued riding. The ranch house came into view and as they rode into the yard the door opened and Marshal Cobb appeared on the veranda, flanked by a couple of Roach's hardcases carrying rifles across their chests. The marshal held some papers in his hand which he commenced to wave in front of Routledge.

'Real nice to see you, Routledge,' he said. 'I sure am pleased you've seen your way to doin' the right thing bringin' these two outlaws in.'

He turned to Carson and Tombstone. 'I have here warrants for your arrest.' he said, 'so throw down your guns and dismount.'

Carson smiled. 'Sorry, Marshal,' he said, 'but we can't oblige.'

'I don't want any trouble,' Cobb retorted, 'but in case you were plannin' on anything, I'd better warn you that the place is surrounded and we have you covered.'

'What are you doin' here, Cobb?' Routledge said. 'How long have you known about this place?'

'That's none of your business,' Cobb replied. 'Now do as I say or I shall have to order my deputies to disarm you.'

The two gunslingers at his side stepped forward and pointed their rifles. For a moment there was a tense silence and then the voice of Tombstone rang out.

'Cobb, you're nothin' but a two-bit skunk. You ain't got the guts to carry this through. And just in case you were aimin' to give your bunch of apes the signal to fire, you'd better be aware I got you covered. One false move and you'll be the first to die.'

Cobb physically blanched.

'Take it easy and think for a moment. These two are wanted men. As a former representative of law and order, I would have thought I'd have your support in puttin' them behind bars.'

Slowly Gillespie dismounted.

'What are you doing?' Cobb shouted.

The two rifles swung in Gillespie's direction as he strode slowly forward.

'Don't make any false moves,' Carson barked. 'Not unless you want to die.'

All eyes were on Gillespie as he stepped on to the veranda. For a moment he stood face to face with Cobb and then slowly he reached out his hand and, taking hold of the marshal's badge pinned to Cobb's shirt, he ripped it from his chest and tossed it into the dirt.

'You don't deserve to wear the badge,' Gillespie snarled.

He turned to the two gunslingers whose rifles were pointed at his chest. 'Best put those things down,' he said.

They glanced at Cobb who was standing open-mouthed with surprise.

'Do as he says!' Carson shouted.

For another moment they remained uncertain before the impasse was broken by the bark of a rifle. One of the Bar X men toppled from his horse, clutching his shoulder. Instantly, there was pandemonium as the others leaped from their horses, seeking shelter as a blaze of gunfire burst over the ranch house yard. A couple of horses went down thrashing, struggling to regain their feet. One of the gunmen backing up Cobb swung his rifle round but Gillespie's gun was already spitting flame and the gunman went reeling backwards, crashing into the wall of the ranch house as blood spurted from his chest. The other gunman started to run and at the same moment Cobb spun round and ran through the partly open door of the ranch house as a hail of gunfire burst from the windows. Gillespie flung himself to the floor and crawled on his hands and knees to a corner of the building behind which he rolled to take temporary shelter. Carson, doubled over, had made it to the corner of the barn and he could see Tombstone behind a water trough. He looked for the others but could not see where they had gone. It was obvious that they were under fire from at least two quarters: from within the building and from the surrounding terrain. Intermingled with the noise of gunfire he could hear the sound of horses and he caught a glimpse of a whole group of riders coming up from the direction of the Big Ooze before they disappeared from sight in the shelter of some trees and bushes which lay just beyond the ranch buildings. He didn't know who had fired the first shot but he guessed it was from one of the newcomers. He could hardly think straight for the cacophony of noise which assailed his ears; it was obvious from the volume of gunfire that they were well outnumbered. Carson guessed what must have happened. Roach and the rest of his gang had arrived, probably leaving the herd behind with just a few of the gunslicks to keep an eye on it.

Suddenly he heard a noise behind him and a bullet kicked up earth close to his left leg. Turning on his back, he saw a gunman leaning out of a barn window. Carson loosed off a shot. The man screamed as a fountain of blood burst from his forehead and he slipped away out of sight. Realizing that there might be others inside, Carson decided to move around to the front of the barn, but a good deal of shooting was coming from that direction. Shouting to Tombstone to cover him he began to run in a crouched position for the door. Bullets slammed into the wood and kicked up dust all around him but he reached his target and, throwing himself through the doorway, hit dirt as someone inside opened fire. It was comparatively dark in the barn and he lay flat, waiting for the next spurt of flame which would tell him where the man was concealed. Slithering forward to the shelter of a bale of straw he looked around him. The barn had an upper storey at the far end which extended part of the way across the building. Light filtered through a hatchway but the ladder had been kicked aside. Carson guessed that his opponent was hiding in the upper section. If he could get to it, Carson reckoned he would have a good vantage point from which to fire down into the ranch house.

Looking up at the aperture and then at the position of the door, Carson reckoned he could make a fair guess at the position of the gunman. It was worth a try. Pointing his six-gun, he pulled the trigger. The bullet crashed through the floorboards and Carson was rewarded with the sound of movement as the gunman jumped up.

Again he fired and this time there was a muted curse and, for a moment, part of the gunman's frame appeared in a corner of the aperture. Carson squeezed the trigger of his gun a third time and from overhead there came a crash as the body of the gunman hit the floor. Carson waited. He could not be sure that the man was not just wounded or faking it. When he was reasonably satisfied that it was safe to move, he ran to the ladder and propping it against the aperture, climbed quickly to the top, his gun at the ready. He was reluctant to raise his head above the opening but there was no need to worry. The man lay prone and it was clear at once that he was dead. Carson moved forward to the window opening and looked out on to a corner of the yard and ranch house. Some horses were lying where they had been shot in the initial burst of gunfire. Tombstone was still sheltering behind the water trough, pinned down but unhurt, and Carson called down to him, partly so that he would not fire in the direction of the barn. Tombstone waved a hand in acknowledgement. Gunfire was still booming from the ranch house and Carson began to return it, aiming through the windows. An answering barrage slammed into the wood around him and he moved back into shelter. He could more or less see where the rest of the Bar X men must be concealed and at one point caught a glimpse of Gillespie as he leaned out from the corner of the ranch house. He couldn't see Routledge or Rik. Some of the Bar X men were firing in the direction of the ranch house but most were aiming towards the surrounding area where Roach and his men were stationed. It was not a good situation and Gillespie, in particular, was dangerously exposed. For the moment he and the rest of the Bar X men could probably hold their own but it was only a question of time before they were outgunned. Something needed to be done, but what? While he was casting about in his mind for inspiration, there came a sudden lull in the battle and then a voice cut through the sporadic gunfire.

'Routledge! Give yourself up!'

Carson tensed. For a few moments there was silence. Carson wondered whether Routledge had been hurt but then to his relief the voice of the rancher rang out in reply.

'If that's you Roach, you can go to hell!'

There came the sound of forced laughter.

'Yeah, this is Roach. I guess you know I'm the owner of the Slash H now. Your time is up, Routledge. I'll give you this one chance to surrender and then get out of the territory.'

Silence descended and Roach's words seem to hang in the air like gun smoke.

'Do you hear me, Routledge? We have the place surrounded. Come out with your hands up and maybe you won't all be killed.'

Again there was silence. Carson was gritting his teeth at the sound of Roach's voice. He decided it was time he took a hand.

'Roach!' he called. 'This is Carson!'

He stopped, not saying any more for the moment. Roach would know all about Carson. His mother would have made sure of that right from Carson's arrival at the Bird Cage. But Roach couldn't be certain of Carson's intentions.

'Carson!' eventually came the reply. 'I don't know who in hell you are or what your game is but you'd better come out now with your hands in the air.'

'Roach, you're scum! How's Cindy? You're OK when it comes to hurtin' young girls but you're up against men now and your ma's not here to help you.' He let that sink in.

'Shut up, Carson! You're a dead man!'

'Collected any scalps lately?' Carson called back.

'I don't know what you mean.'

'Oh, I think you do. Young girls and old men, that's just about your style, isn't it Roach? Remember an old-time prospector back in Silver Junction! You killed him and took his money. You've never given him a thought, have you? That was your mistake, Roach. He's back again to haunt you and right now it's payback time.'

'I don't know what the hell you're on about, Carson, but I've just about had enough of you.'

'What you gonna do without your ma, Roach? She ain't here right now. And I don't think she'd really approve if she knew everything you've been up to.'

'I told you to shut up, Carson!' Roach screamed. 'You've had your chance. Now you're goin' to die. All of you.'

'We're ready and waitin' Roach!'

Carson allowed a grim flicker of a smile to cross his face. They were up against it, but somehow he felt a new confidence. He jammed bullets into the chambers of his six-guns and faced the window as the place burst into a fresh round of gunfire. Drawing a bead on the nearest window of the ranch house he began to shoot. Tombstone was blazing away below him while bullets ripped all around, churning up the water in the basin and ricocheting from the sides of the trough. Carson had to make a choice now. The upper part of the barn was a useful place from which to fire on the ranch house but the position was getting difficult to maintain and he was in danger of becoming pinned down like Tombstone and Gillespie. He needed to do something which might serve to break the deadlock.

Climbing down the ladder, he ran to the back of the building where the gunfire was more sporadic and, poking his head out, took a good look around. There was not much to see, just an empty corral with a broken-down wagon and back of it some rough ground leading to a patch of trees. Standing among them, however, were three horses which must have bolted at the commencement of the shooting. A plan began to form in his head and he moved cautiously away from the shelter of the barn. As he did so a shot rang out from the trees and he fell to the ground, still triggering his gun. He caught a glimpse of someone; it was Rik Routledge who must have had a similar idea to Carson and made his own way towards the back of the ranch house.

'It's me, Carson!' he yelled.

Crouching low, he ran across to the corral, vaulting the fence before crashing into the cover of the trees. Rik's gun was blazing in an effort to cover his run but there seemed to be little return fire.

'You sure got to that no-good hombre with your comments,' Rik said with a grin.

Carson looked at him. It was incredible, but he seemed to be actually enjoying the situation. Maybe it was just the adrenalin coursing through his veins.

'We need to do something quick,' Carson said. 'I don't know about the rest of them, but Tombstone and Gillespie are in some trouble.'

'Sure. What you got in mind?'

'Seems to me we need to get in the rear of those varmints. At present, they got us pinned down. Why don't you and me try to work our way round without bein' seen and come at them from behind?'

'It's risky,' Rik replied, 'but we gotta try something.'

'We'll take the horses and ride in a wide circuit and hope to take them by surprise.'

Without further ado they crept up to the horses. Tightening the cinches, they climbed into leather. Leaving the third horse in the shelter of the trees, they edged their way to the far side of the corral and began to ride fast in the opposite direction to the fighting.

'I don't like this,' Rik remarked. 'Feel like I'm runnin' away.'

They continued to ride till Carson was satisfied that they were well beyond being seen by any of Roach's men.

'We'll come at 'em from two different points,' Carson said. 'Make sure you ride a wide loop. Keep out of sight. Wait till you hear my signal. I'll fire two quick shots and then a third. Then make a noise. They might think there's more of us.'

They heeled round and started to ride in a circle, Rik to the right and Carson to the left, before straightening up and continuing to ride hard. From time to time Carson could see Rik and then he would disappear below a dip in the ground. The sounds of conflict grew louder again and they could both see plumes of smoke from where the gunmen were concealed behind rocks and clumps of trees. Raising his gun, Carson fired; two shots in rapid succession and then a third. Instantly gunfire burst from his right and Rik came into view once more, blazing away. Carson was firing rapidly and started whooping. Some of the gunmen, taken by surprise, burst from cover; two of them went reeling to the ground. Others began to return fire. Bringing his horse to a sliding halt, Carson jumped from the saddle and took up a position behind some bushes. He could not see what had happened to Rik but gunfire continued to sound from his direction.

Working his way through the scrub, Carson was able to get a good line on a group of the gunslicks and his fire was effective. A further crescendo of gunfire came from the direction of the ranch and Carson took heart that his friends were still giving as good as they got. A shot winged uncomfortably close and he looked about for another position. As he did so, he became aware of movement behind him. Off in the distance a fresh batch of riders had appeared and Carson's stomach sank. If Roach was able to bring up more men, they were doomed. The riders were coming on fast and, as they approached, Carson prepared to fight them off as best he could. They were kicking up a good deal of dust but as they got nearer Carson thought he recognized one or two of them and then the realization dawned that they were not Roach's gunslicks but some of the Bar X men who had been left behind when the rest of them had gone after the herd. As if that wasn't enough, he now saw that among them was the unmistakable figure of Laura Routledge. As they came up they began to fire and then, dismounting, they sought cover themselves. Bullets whistled over Carson's head and kicked up dirt nearby from a different direction and he realized that they were from the Bar X men who had mistaken him for one of the gunslicks. Above the roar of gunfire he shouted to them, trying to make them realize their mistake, but it was impossible to tell in all the commotion whether his words had been heard or not. It made little difference, for suddenly there was a surge from the direction of the ranch and a group of Roach's men came into view. They had taken to their horses. Carson directed his fire towards them but they had veered away and were already too difficult a target. Carson couldn't be sure whether they were making their escape or whether they were attempting a move to circumvent the newcomers. The firing from immediately in front of him had dwindled. Either the gunmen hidden there were dead or had shifted their position.

Carson moved forward, keeping close to the ground, until he reached a point where he could see the area from where the gunmen had been directing their fire. There were several bodies lying in contorted positions but no sign of anyone still left. Carson advanced a little further and raised himself up. He had a view of the ranch and not much shooting seemed to be coming from it. The hint of a grin crossed his face. It seemed that for the moment, at least, they had the better of the fight and his thoughts were confirmed as the sound of galloping hoofs came to his ears followed by a further burst of gunfire from behind him. More of Roach's men had decided to leave and been met with a response. Suddenly a shot rang out and he felt a sharp searing pain across his shoulder. Looking up, he saw a man astride his horse with his rifle raised. Carson rolled aside as he fired again, the bullet kicking up dirt where he had been, and then the man dug his spurs into the side of his horse and began to ride away. Carson had only a brief moment to look at his assailant but it was enough for him to recognize the ugly leering countenance of Wesley Roach. Ignoring the pain in his shoulder and the possibility of being hit by further bullets, Carson got to his feet and began to run back to where he had left his horse. Springing to the saddle, he set off in pursuit. Bullets whined around him — he couldn't tell whether they were from friend or enemy. His instincts told him that Roach's bullet had done little more than graze his shoulder. It would take a worse injury to stop him now. Leaving the battle at the ranch to take care of itself, confident that they had just about won the day, he gritted his teeth against pain and urged his horse forward.

Roach had a decent start on him but Carson had him in his sights and his horse was running smoothly. He had the feeling he was slowly gaining. It soon became obvious that Roach was heading for the Big Ooze and Carson felt sure that he was aware he was being pursued. He saw few signs of other riders. The gunslicks appeared to have scattered without any definite aim. Perhaps some of them would be gathered at the river or maybe they would keep on riding till they reached the Slash H.

For a long time the two of them kept riding, the distance between them slowly diminishing, till Carson eased the Appaloosa's run, slowing him to a walk so that he could take a blow. After a time he rode on again. There was no immediate sign of Roach but presently he came into sight once more. Carson figured that if Roach was to make a move, it would be when he reached the river where the trees would offer shelter and the possibility of an ambush.

He came down towards the river late in the afternoon. He had lost sight of Roach again but he guessed he would probably be lying in wait. Instead of continuing to ride straight ahead, he veered off once he saw the line of trees indicating the presence of the Big Ooze. When he was satisfied that he was well out of sight of watching eyes and a long way further down stream, he turned and rode down through the trees till he could see the waters of the river blinking in the late afternoon sunlight. The river was running more quickly than previously but even so it presented no obstacle to a crossing. Emerging from the water, the horse snickered and shied. There was something lying in the water's edge and, glancing down, Carson saw that it was the remains of one of the gunmen shot in the previous encounter by the stream. It must have been carried on a slow current to this point. There wasn't much left of what had once been a man.

Carson carried on riding till he judged he had reached a point not far below where Roach would have emerged on the river bank on the opposite side. Dismounting, he tied the horse to a tree. Taking his rifle from its scabbard, he continued on foot, looking closely for signs of anyone on either bank or for indications of a rider having crossed the river. He wasn't sure just what to expect but his precautions were rewarded when he came upon a tethered horse. He had a hunch it belonged to Roach. If so, then Roach had to be somewhere near. Any further consideration of the matter was quickly ended when a voice from behind him snapped: 'Throw down your gun!'

Cursing inwardly, Carson did as he was told.

'Unbuckle your gunbelt and let it drop.'

For a moment Carson considered making a move but as if in answer the voice snarled: 'Don't think about it. One false move and I'll break your spine.'

Carson let his gunbelt drop to the ground. For a moment there was silence and then out of the trees stepped four of Roach's gunslicks. Carson felt the tip of a rifle pressed against his back.

'Figured you might turn up,' one of them said. 'Start walkin'.'

Carson had no choice but to obey. As they walked, the gunslicks laughed and joked and all the time Carson was conscious of the rifle at his back. Presently they arrived at a clearing among the trees. Standing there was another group of men among whom Carson recognized Marshal Cobb and, standing slightly apart, another figure with an evil sneer spread across its countenance. It was Wesley Roach. At the back of the clearing stood a tree slightly isolated from the rest and over a lower branch hung a rope. A horse stood beneath it. Carson was pushed forward and as he stumbled he was seized from behind. Roach stepped forward. He spat on the ground and then without warning he punched Carson heavily in the stomach. Carson crumpled but was prevented from falling by the men who held him. Another blow struck him hard across the face.

'I don't know what your game is,' Roach hissed. 'But one way and another you've put me to a lot of trouble.'

'That's nothin' to what you got comin',' Carson managed to reply.

'I don't think you're in any position to be making threats,' Roach snarled. Drawing his arm back, he delivered another punch to Carson's midriff. Carson hung, winded and feeling sick, in the grasp of Roach's henchmen, awaiting the next blow.

'I think I've had about as much of you as I can take,' Roach continued. He leaned forward and, taking the end of the rope suspended from the tree branch, he fastened it round Carson's neck.

'OK boys, hoist him up,' he ordered.

Two of the gunslicks lifted Carson on to the horse's back. Carson could see no way out of the situation. It seemed his time had come.

'Roach!' he grunted. 'I'll see you in hell.'

Roach emitted a mocking hollow laugh.

'This is sure turnin' out to be some party!' one of the gunmen commented.

'Why not scalp him right now?' another said. 'Why wait till he's dead?'

'Don't worry, boys,' Roach said. 'I'm makin' sure this is goin' to be one real slow hangin'.'

Carson reached up a hand. The noose seemed slack about his neck.

'Ain't gonna do you no good,' another gunslick commented.

Carson began to drop his arms before suddenly reaching up and grabbing the rope. At the same moment there came a barrage of gunfire from the trees and then there was total confusion. The horse bolted, leaving Carson clinging to the rope in a desperate effort to prevent it strangling him. There were bodies strewing the ground and, out the corner of his eye, Carson could see Roach running full tilt towards the river. A single shot rang out from nearby and Carson came crashing to the ground, landing heavily with the noose still fastened round his neck. He scrambled to his feet as someone came running up with a knife in his hand. Carson rolled over, prepared to fight for his life, but it was the face of Tombstone which was grinning down into his own. With a couple of cuts, Tombstone severed the rope.

'You sure know how to leave things till the last moment,' Carson gasped.

'You can thank Miss Laura for that shot,' Tombstone replied. 'She's sure one mean markswoman with a derringer.'

Carson rose to his knees and glanced about him in confusion. The firing had subsided. Other people were running up and he was looking for Laura.

'Where is she?' he mumbled.

In another moment his senses cleared. 'Roach!' he gasped.

Without further explanation he was on his feet and running fast towards the river. His body was bruised and aching and his shoulder hurt where the bullet had grazed it but he felt a wave of energy course through him as he searched for Roach. He was still somewhat confused but realized that Roach would probably make for his horse. He was at the riverbank now and he looked desperately up and down for any sign of Roach. Through the trees a little further off, the figure of the gunslick suddenly emerged, moving towards Carson. At first Roach did not notice him but as soon as he did so he plunged into the water. Carson ran a little way and then threw himself into the river after him. A shot whistled close to his head and then another. Roach had drawn his six-gun and was firing at him. Without pausing, Carson continued to splash through the water in hot pursuit. All at once the river shelved and the water was around Carson's waist. Ahead of him, Roach stumbled, firing off another shot as the gun slipped from his fingers. He was half wading, half swimming now. Acting like a man possessed, Carson was gaining on him. They were both swimming and then, as they began to approach the opposite shore, the riverbed rose and they were stumbling again through the shallows. Roach reached for his other gun but Carson was upon him, throwing himself forward and catching him around the legs. They went over in the shallow water, Carson's hand clutching at Roach's gun arm. For a few moments the issue was in doubt as Roach desperately sought to free himself of his opponent's grasp and bring the gun into play, but Carson forced his arm back until Roach's fingers reluctantly gave up their grasp of the weapon and it fell into the water. Roach struggled to regain his feet but Carson held him and they both fell. Roach's fingers were round Carson's neck but Carson managed to prise them apart and then he slugged Roach hard in the face. Roach staggered back as Carson delivered another blow. Roach sank to his knees as Carson's fists continued to pummel him in a blind fury of rage and hatred. Beneath the rain of blows, Roach's body went limp until at last Carson registered the fact. Ceasing the onslaught, he dragged Roach up out of the water and deposited him on the bank of the river. For a few moments they both lay there and then Roach's eyes opened. He was breathing heavily and his face was a battered pulp.

'Please, Carson!' he pleaded.

Carson rose to his feet and looked down at him. Finally he had Roach at his mercy but even as he regarded the limp form of his enemy all thoughts of revenge suddenly leaked away. All at once he had a vision of himself and Laura the day they had declared their love for one another. He looked up and there she was on the other side of the river. A couple of Bar X men were with her, and wading through the shallows on this side was Tombstone.

'Please!' the suppliant voice of Roach continued to whine as Tombstone came alongside, putting his arm around Carson and lending him support. 'Remember that old man now?' Carson said to Roach.

Roach's eyes were blank.

'People called him Pack Rat. Well, I guess I'm a kind of pack rat too, bringin' you somethin' in exchange for what you took.'

Roach continued to stare with blind incomprehension.

'No, I guess you wouldn't remember,' Carson continued. 'What's one old timer among all the rest? But he did me a real favour. I owed him.'

Carson glanced again towards the river. Laura was being helped across by the two Bar X men. With a final contemptuous glance at the cringing figure on the riverbank, he broke free of Tombstone's supporting arm and turned to meet her.

Tombstone looked down at the

prostrate form of Wesley Roach. The man was sobbing as he continued to grovel and beg for mercy.

'Well,' Tombstone said, more to himself than anyone else, 'I guess that's one old timer he'd have done better to leave alone.'

We do hope that you have enjoyed reading this large print book.

Did you know that all of our titles are available for purchase?

We publish a wide range of high quality large print books including:
Romances, Mysteries, Classics General Fiction Non Fiction and Westerns

Special interest titles available in large print are:
The Little Oxford Dictionary Music Book, Song Book Hymn Book, Service Book

Also available from us courtesy of Oxford University Press:
Young Readers' Dictionary (large print edition) Young Readers' Thesaurus (large print edition)

For further information or a free brochure, please contact us at:
Ulverscroft Large Print Books Ltd., The Green, Bradgate Road, Anstey, Leicester, LE7 7FU, England. Tel: (00 44) **0116 236 4325 Fax:** (00 44) **0116 234 0205**

Other titles in the
Linford Western Library:

HELL FIRE IN PARADISE

Chuck Tyrell

Laurel Baker lost her husband and her two boys on the same day. Then, menacingly, logging magnate Robert Dunn rides into her ranch on Paradise Creek to buy her out. Laurel refuses as her loved ones are buried there — prompting Dunn to try shooting to get his way. Laurel's friends stick by her, but will their loyalty match Dunn's ten deadly gunmen? And in the final battle for her land, can she live through hell fire in Paradise?

THE BLACK MOUNTAIN DUTCHMAN

Steve Ritchie

In Wyoming, when Maggie Buckner is captured by a gang of outlaws, 'the Dutchman' is the only one who can free her. Near Savage Peak, the old man adjusts the sights on his Remington No. 1 rifle as the riders come into range. When he stops shooting, three of the captors lay dead. After striking the first deadly blows, the Dutchman trails the group across South Pass like the fourth horseman of the apocalypse . . . and surely Hell follows with him.

THE FIGHTING MAN

Alan Irwin

Young Rob Sinclair, a homesteader's son in the Wyoming Territory, has never handled a gun. But when the Nolan gang kills his parents, he's determined to bring the culprits to justice. Against the prevailing knowledge that only a real fighting man could defeat the Nolan gang, Rob learns to fight and sets out to search for the killers. He eventually reaches the Texas Panhandle, little knowing what awaits him there. Can he complete such a perilous mission alone?

BLOOD FEUD

John Dyson

Higo, a Japanese railroad worker, kills two guards and escapes into Utah's canyonlands, and when Cal Mitchell goes after him — it's not just for the $500 reward . . . Along with his tempestuous passion for Modesty, dark secrets beckon Cal homeward, towards the mountains of Zion. He also seeks vengeance against the five Granger brothers. Blood flows and bullets fly as Cal steps back into his murky past. Can he find peace when the odds are stacked against him?